STAR SEED NATION

ASCENSION INTO 5D

SHAR VEDA

-For the intuitive young leaders of the world brave enough to make decisions based on love.

ABOUT THE AUTHOR

Shar Veda ALC, AYT is an Ayurveda Lifestyle Counselor, Ayurveda Yoga Therapist, healer, writer, and channel. Her specialties are intuitive counsel, Ayurveda + 5 elements, women's health, and sustainable high-vibration beauty, self-care + ritual for personal and planetary ascension.

A graduate of Pennsylvania State University, California College of Ayurveda, American Institute of Vedic Studies, and Vedic Conservatory, Shar has worked in both wellness and publishing for over 20 years.

In that time, she has served as healer at large for several affluent communities, as health counselor in two girls houses for at risk teens, as yoga therapist to homeless and low income kids, as trusted confidante to elite private clients, and as writer for countless high-vibration beauty and wellness brands in articles for national magazines.

Born on a Mother's Day new moon just outside Philadelphia, Pennsylvania, United States of America with gifts of clairvoyance, claircognizance, and clairaudience, Shar has been honored to study, travel and work closely with leaders in healing arts from many traditions in many lands. However, her own healing powers are lifetimes old, derived from Celtic lineage dating back to the house of Ulster and still not fully realized.

Shar Veda offers counseling and healing for women of all ages using Ayurveda, astrology, ESP and channeling. You can find her at Sharveda.com

NOTE FROM THE AUTHOR

Lena the main character of *Star Seed Nation: Ascension into 5D* was born in Wilmington, North Carolina during the Venus retrograde of 2012. The book was originally set to be about an intuitive teen girl from a long line of women seers and healers, reconnecting with her dead Grandma and welcoming the elements in a sort of Rite of Passage.

At that time, my health and wellness business, teen daughter, and maintaining my own physical and mental health in North Carolina was all I could handle. I was unable to give the project the attention it deserved then and timing is important, so I put it down a few years.

Three years later, however, when I moved to Southern Oregon, 75 miles north of Mount Shasta, California, January 2015, I picked up a channel that insisted on being included.

The time was right!

Inner Earth, Galactic Council, political agenda, and extreme weather poured forth. I simply (!?) allowed myself to be guided into the daily ritual of automatic writing and whole new scenes were birthed. The next step for me was semi-isolation for two years to turn the visual and audio channel flow I received in abundance at light speed, into enjoyable chapters with structure for readers to enjoy.

For me the channel I picked up near Mount Shasta, is not so much about "full disclosure" like it is for many others, it's about what Earth Root Chakra wanted to communicate.

The time for re-calibration in NOW!

ONE

It's 7:30AM and 85 degrees already. I'm on the back deck sipping an iced mocha with chocolate hemp milk, watching Kiki Astromatrix' special astrology forecast on Uranus at the 29th degree of Taurus for the tenth time this week.

In my natal chart, I have Uranus at 29 degrees, the intuition degree, in my 8th house. My moon and sun are in Taurus in the 3rd house and I am Aquarius rising, whose modern ruler is Uranus.

So I know big changes are coming for me and I am trying to figure out when and what. At fifteen, I am a fairly good astrologer but I haven't mastered it. There is a lot to know, and the more I learn the more I realize how infinite it is.

Kiki Astromatrix, the astrologer I follow, is always spot on with her forecasts. Twenty something with a cool accent and great hair, Kiki usually films her forecasts in the Australian outback in

either her Earth dome or native plant garden. She is traveling this year though. So, it's different every time.

"As you all know my astro-family, it takes seven years for Uranus to transit through a sign. Every planet is different, remember? If you are taking my online class you should have the transit times memorized by now. Numbers and cycles are soooo important!" Kiki says adjusting her gold pyramid shaped glasses.

"Ok. Let's pull up the chart so you can see. There," she says circling the Uranus glyph that looks like an antennae on top of a globe. "Uranus is in the 28th degree of Taurus now... eeking towards Gemini. Uranus, the modern ruler of Aquarius and astrology, rules revolutionary vision, lightning bolt insight, electricity, inventions, the future, technology, artificial intelligence, progressive change, and alien life forms."

Pausing dramatically to look skywards, Kiki brushes glossy black bangs behind her ear. "His transit through the stable fixed sign of Taurus, for those of you who are just tuning in, which rules planet Earth, money, financial systems, luxury items, agriculture, and real estate has already brought drastic changes to these areas since his ingress in Taurus on May 15th, 2018, right? We've all seen some stuff." she laughs.

"When Uranus reaches the critical 29th degree of Taurus, *radical change is going shock the world*. If you have major placements in either Aquarius or Taurus, like your rising, sun or moon, even your Venus or Mars, be ready for sudden, unexpected change. Your entire world is ... going ... to ... be... rocked."

Kiki leans into the camera, her wise dark eyes fringed with long turquoise lashes. "Stay open Star Seeds and ready to receive. I want you all to write in and tell me what changes are happening for you and when. Exact timing is helpful. This is history in the making, my loves. Until next time! Be bold, be brave, be you!"

Kiki Astromatrix blows a kiss, puckering her bright blue lips and waving goodbye to her fandom. Kiko her German Shepherd, stands up in the background and the cam clicks off as the big dog pads over, wagging its tail. A sport tampon commercial pops up and I close my laptop, sliding it into its purple case.

Clang!! David, my older brother, kicks the back gate open with his foot. Dripping salt water and holding a surfboard under his arm, he leans his sandy board against the fence next to two others and walks around the near empty pool towards me.

"Why do you waste your time with that astro shit, dork?" he demands standing in front of me shaking his shoulder length blonde hair.

"Wait," I say squinting one eye and touching my cheek, the classic confused expression, "*You* are worried about *me* wasting time? The guy who got held back a year because he refused to do homework? You don't think redoing eleventh grade is a bigger waste of time?"

David's tan face reddens and he turns around sticking his butt directly in front of my face.

"Right. Well, don't take it personally. I'm takin' this wet suit off right here so I don't waste any more of my time."

"David! Do that in your room!" I squeeze my eyes shut. "Nah, rather do it here. Hang those up for me will ya?" He says tossing his wet shorts on top of my head and walking into the house buff naked.

"Ughhh! You idiot!" I scream throwing his shorts after him and hitting him in the back.

"You want me to turn around?" "No!"

"Then, hang 'em up." "Fine! Just *go*."

I squeeze the swim shorts out over the pool and walk over to the clothesline on one corner of the fence where three more pair of David's surf trunks hang stiff with dried salt.

"You need a ride today, dork?" He yells from his bedroom window.

"No, Sierra's Mom is picking me up," I yell back clipping a clothespin on the folded over waistband of his shorts. "They're having a last day of school party at her house. I might sleep over after."

"Am I invited?"

"It's for tenth grade graduates only, David."

"Even better."

"Dude, you are seriously warped."

Beep. Beep.

Sierra's Mom is out front.

Throwing a disgusted look in David's general direction, I run to collect my laptop and backpack, then let myself out the back gate.

A moist, salty breeze whips my long hair around catching it in the iron latch then tangling it momentarily in my mouth as I pull the gate closed behind me.

Our house is a block from the ocean and it gets windy. We live in Wrightsville Beach, North Carolina in a two-story home. It's a great location if you like water, which I do. You can't see the ocean from the lawn or front porch but you can hear it.

My parents have a good view of the ocean from their bedroom though and David and I can see the bay from ours, his and my separate rooms, I mean, we don't share one.

One trapped blonde hair waving from the clutches of the gate latch shows which way the wind is blowing as I turn on my heel and jog to the white SUV waiting to take me to school.

"Hey, Lena!" Sierra greets me as I climb in the backseat.

"Hi Lena," says Sierra's Mom.

"Hey girl," Naia, our other friend, says. "Hi guys! Last day of school!"

"Are you excited now? Yesterday you were all upset you have to go to the mountains."

"I mean," I say sliding my seatbelt on and depositing my back-pack between my knees, "it'll be nice to be outta school awhile but ya I still don't wanna go. My grandmom's dead so it's weird we're even going this year, right?"

"Weird," Sierra nods, dark eyes flashing in agreement.

"Werd," Naia seconds nodding her strawberry blond head and

making a pie-eyed fish face. She snaps a photo of herself and uploads it somewhere.

"Last day of school pics! Lean in!"

We lean in with smiles and peace signs. My eyes are closed in most of them but at least one is good.

"Erase the worst ones, please," Sierra says, "and send me the best."

Sierra's mom laughs, "So what's the big news in astrology this week, Lena?"

"Well," I clear my throat. "There is big news..."

"Ugh. Always. Here we go. The astrology channel," Sierra says irritated. "Not everyone in this car wants to hear about it..."

TWO

Six hours later, school is out and summer has officially started. Naia, Sierra and I are in bathing suits in Sierra's backyard. All five pool umbrellas are up creating a large triangle of shade, the recycled waterfall feature is on, and a robotic disc cleaner is circling the three feet of rainwater in the infinity shaped pool.

Non-Extinct Wildlife, our party theme this year, hangs in a colorful banner over the waterfall with a pouncing cheetah on one side and a splashing seal on the other. In between them are the words, *Congratulations Graduates,* with letters written in various animal print.

"Remember when we could fill our pools all the way and like take baths every night if we wanted to?" Naia yells over the roar of the air pump.

She is pumping up a giant sea horse floaty to go with its already pumped up friends, an alligator, dolphin, and shark. Her long strawberry blond hair is up in a high bun. She is wearing a black tankini and covered in pink and yellow sunscreen.

"We were nine, right?" I yell back. "I used to love diving for rings and floating."

"Ohmygosh, I miss taking baths!" Sierra chimes in from the outdoor kitchen.

"Me too. I totally miss baths! It's still better here than the west coast though. California water rations are like ten gallons a day now. That means you drink some, take a one-minute shower, and if you're lucky, wash the dishes or do a load of laundry. Water gets shut off after that."

"Whaaaa?"

"But I mean who even drinks tap water anymore..."

"Right?"

We sigh wistfully remembering when we had enough water to do whatever we wanted with...fill our pools, take baths, jump through sprinklers. Now we have to be like really creative and water restrictions are getting harsher every year even on the east coast.

"So like do you at least get to do the two week theatre camp jawn this summer?" Naia asks changing the subject like she always does jumping from one topic to the next without transition. She has a lot of Aquarius in her and we're all used to her mobile attention span.

"No," I say walking towards the outdoor kitchen where Sierra, a

Virgo rising has just finished pouring fruit juice into popsicle molds.

"Why?" Sierra probes, "Acting could be like a *career* for you. You're really good at it." Hopping up on the counter, swinging her tan legs, she kicks off white leather sandals to examine a mosquito bite on her ankle. "Naia and I are going to soccer camp and I'm not even that good. You should go to theatre camp. I mean, it's what you do, right?"

I nod. "My father has a pipe dream I'll do something in the family business when I graduate though," I say sourly.

"What, like be a lawyer?"

"Mmmm ...more like anything to do with the companies they invest in. My father's side of the family is *all big business*... so investing, promoting, defending, sales...you know, things like that. It's all tied together. And David is pretty much a lost cause so ... all eyes are on me. Did you know he failed this year?"

"No way!" Sierra and Naia gasp in unison.

"Dude, so he's gotta do eleventh grade over?" Naia asks. "We'll all be in the same grade?! That is so weird."

"Yep and probably on purpose too, to like to get back at my parents for pressuring him or something."

"Smart one," Naia says rolling her hazel eyes. "Throw your future away to get back at your parents."

"Like our future's sooo stable," Sierra snorts sarcastically. "Maybe David's the smart one...enjoying himself while he can. I mean the world could end any day with like a major natural disaster or some... world leader having a bad day."

"Or we could run out of water..." I add snowballing off Sierra.

"Ohmygosh, people. Don't be so negative!" Naia says sharply shaking her head.

"We're not being so negative, we're being so realistic. Ever watch the news?"

"The fake news, you mean?"

"Guys!" I yell, face palming my forehead. "I am not up for a political debate today!" I say exhaling irritably. "Who's coming tonight?" It's my turn to change the topic.

"Oh just...everybody who's anybody in our grade. Most of the people from soccer, football, debate, and volleyball..." Sierra says jumping off the counter slipping back into her flip-flops. "I invited some people from theatre too ...for you," she smiles flittering her long eyelashes.

"Gaston's mixing tonight, right? So we can dance our butts off?" Naia laughs coming up behind me hugging me and pressing pink and yellow sunscreen all over my back.

"Hey! You got pink cheetah stripes all over me!" I say twisting around to look.

"Cheetah's have spots smarty. I'm a tiger," Naia raises her eyebrows, makes her hands into claws. "Roar," she says slashing the air inches away from my face.

I laugh. "Oh right, a tiger. But I don't want stripes. I've decided... I want stars. Can you do that?"

"What kind of animal has stars?" "Uuuummm ... a galactimal?" I giggle.

"Ohmygosh, never tell that joke again!"

"Was it that bad?"

"Dumb as shit, gurl," Naia says. Sierra seconds this nodding vigorously.

"Ok. No more bad jokes today," I promise, "*if* you make me an animal from another planet. May I please have stars?" I ask politely making prayer hands and an angel face.

"Everybody knows you're from another planet already," Sierra says rolling her eyes. "You talk about astrology *like all the time*. Why don't you try being on this planet tonight?"

"Oh, let her be," says Naia jabbing Sierra with an elbow. "You can have stars. What color? I'll get the stuff."

"I think blue... and *gold* or maybe turquoise and gold."

"I have turquoise and yellow. Will that work?"

"Hmm," Sierra says studying the tubes of sunscreen. "If you mix brown and yellow you might get gold."

Naia bends over the colors squeezing yellow and brown onto a plate biting her lip in concentration. The mix turns out pretty good.

"I like it. Go for it," I say settling back in the lounge chair, legs crossed at the ankles.

Having someone paint you is more relaxing than a pedicure or massage. My grandmom used to do it for David and me when we were little. Body painting should be a therapy.

While Naia turns me into a sunscreen based galactic animal, I pull *YouTube* up on my phone and put ear buds in. A *Star Seed Nation Alert* pops up as "recommended for you." I click and listen relaxing as Naia paints me ankles to wrists with gold brown smudges and turquoise stars.

In that place between sleep and awake, where total relaxation is, the following alert ambles into the deepest part of my brain in a soothing computerized female voice.

"Earth is ascending. The purification process, what humans call 'extreme weather', is preparing the planet and its inhabitants for her new position in the fifth dimension.

To increase the chances of human survival during this process, The Galactic Council is stepping in, actively recruiting high vibration young people known throughout the galaxy as "New Earth Star Seeds" to join mission NEAR. *New Earth Advanced Recalibration.*

The mission itself while simple in nature requires a large team of high frequency youth to Implement. New Earth Star Seeds will naturally be drawn to the recruitment. If you are listening to this message, chances are you are a Star Seed.

Other signs you are a Star Seed include extreme sensitivity to and refusal to absorb violence in any form including entertainment and news. Extreme sensitivity to chemicals, pharmaceuticals, alcohol and drugs, questioning authority when something doesn't seem right, a feeling that you are a part of something greater than daily life, a feeling that you have not always lived on Earth, being a big picture thinker, caring immensely about the planet and all of life, possessing a sixth sense, having an ancestor with a sixth sense, and or having an ancestor who has been in contact with Extraterrestrials are all signs that you are a New Earth Star Seed.

If you are a person born in the 21st century with three or more of these qualifications, the Galactic Council is looking for you! Two seats urgently need filled in the United States chapter of the GC. Two seats... ask yourself, could one be yours? Star Seed youth, step to the calling now."

The message plays around and around on a loop while Naia paints me on the lounge chair in the triangle of shade. White light from the sun reflecting on pool water dances behind my eyes and maybe I see an image of light beings in a circle, waiting...for me?

WHEN I WAKE up I am alone by the pool, covered in colored sunscreen. The sun has moved beyond the umbrella shade and I am fully in it. Groggy, I peel myself off the lounge chair and go inside.

Naia and Sierra are in Sierra's room.

"Heyyyyy!" I say looking in the vanity mirror shaking the vision of light beings out of my head. "I like it! But you only did my front can you do my back now?" I garble a bit dazed from sleeping in the hot Carolina sun.

"You fell asleep dude so you can be half a space animal now.

I don't have time to finish you. People are gonna be here soon and I still have to get ready," Naia says taking out her bun, shaking her long hair out. "Toss me that brush?"

Sierra tosses her the brush. Naia starts brushing out her long hair.

"Besides, she can't really paint your back because then you'd have to stand all night. My mom would kill you if you got colored sunscreen all over her furniture," Sierra mandates penciling in her already perfect brows in front of the wall mirror.

"Oh ya," I say sitting on the bed. "That makes sense. I don't wanna stand all night..."

"Are you drinking tonight?" Naia asks. "You should. Let loose a little. It's your last night here. Mika's brother is bringing beer and Yuna is bringing wine."

"Your mom is letting you have alcohol?"

"She doesn't know dummy! We're keeping it in the room." "We have vodka here now if you want some."

"No thanks, I think I'm allergic to vodka," I say scrunching my nose in distaste. "Because the one time I drank like screwdrivers or something at a wedding, I threw up and had a really bad headache for over 24 hours."

"That's why you sip pinky up girl," Naia laughs making the pinky up gesture with her hand and tipping her head back. "One drink lasts you a whole night like that."

"Are you sleeping over?" Sierra asks brushing her shiny gold brown hair out upside down.

"I don't know yet," I say admiring myself in the mirror. Naia is totally artistic and I look exactly how I wanted. I am a starry turquoise and gold space cat now. "You did a great job with the stars and whiskers on my face, Nai."

"Thanks, I try."

"The front of you is like a space cat and the back is like you slept on a lounge chair for an hour! All these indents..." Sierra laughs running her finger up my spine.

Knock knock.

Clarie and Yuna, the official cool girl duo walk in and plop down on the bed smug looks on both of their pretty faces.

"Hello, Hello ladies," Yuna smiles patting her heavy designer backpack.

"Did you bring wine," Naia asks bouncing up and down, mascara wand and mirror in her hands.

"Yes, I did!" Yuna smiles self-satisfied, "*and champagne*!! My mom is in so many wine clubs she won't even *know* the difference. I've taken stuff pah-lenty of times."

"Ooh champagne!" Naia purrs happily applying pink mascara to match her tiger stripes. "Let's have some."

"It's nice to drink champagne like out of flute glasses though, you know those skinny wine glasses? Do you have any of those, Sierra?"

"We do but my Mom will notice if we use them. She won't let us drink obviously... so we have to hide it in my room and go back and forth unless we mix it in plastic cups. Even then she might do a taste test..."

Yuna and Clarie wrinkle their perfect noses.

"Yuck. Champagne in plastic. Nothing tastes good in plastic."

"I know right," Sierra shrugs, "but that's what we gotta do."

"Ya, we're fifteen, really not supposed to be drinking *at all yet*," I say kind of wishing I didn't as soon as it leaves me mouth.

Yuna laughs haughtily, "Well some of us are a *mature multicultural 15*. My mother is from France and she says in France, kids our age *and younger* drink wine with their meals, it's no big deal. I happen to appreciate a fine wine," Yuna says primly looking me up and down.

"What's with all the stars?"

"I'm a galact..."

Naia covers my mouth with her hand before I can finish. "Nope, that joke is not allowed! She's a ... a space cat."

"Yes. She is," Yuna sneers rolling her eyes.

"I painted her," Naia says. "I think she looks good!"

"It's good artwork but... pretty fuckin' juvenile. Whatever. I for one will not be painting myself," says Clarie standing to apply silvery peach lipstick in the vanity mirror.

"Hey, girl, you do you! Everybody else is already taken."

Clarie rolls her eyes at Naia and presses her freshly lipsticked lips together. She smiles at herself in the mirror rubbing a little lipstick off her tooth.

"So, we gonna do this or what? People gonna be here soon! Let's have a pre-game toast. Pop that cork, lady!" Naia says dancing around Yuna.

"I like the way you think, girl," Yuna says winking at Naia. "Have you ever opened a bottle of champagne?"

All four of us shake our heads as Yuna pulls out a large green bottle of Brut Rose champagne with a white and gold label.

"Then you're in for a treat," Yuna laughs a tinkling fake-ish laugh. Throwing her head back she holds the bottle up like a magician making sure we all get a good look.

We watch impressed as Yuna expertly takes the wrapper off,

twists the little silver tab, and with the cork in between her finger and thumb commands, "Stand clear everyone, this thing pops! And get a cup ready in case it spills."

Naia scrambles for and holds out a blue plastic cup, "ready." Yuna nods.

Pop! The cork shoots across the room and lands with a 'tink' in Sierra's fish tank.

"Hells ya! We shoulda filmed that shit! It landed in the fucking fish tank!" Clarie yells clutching her stomach and flop- ping back on the bed.

Naia shoots a quick video of the cork floating in the tank with everyone laughing like crazy before Sierra fishes it out.

"That *was* awesome," Sierra laughs throwing the cork in the trash can. "Yuna for president!"

Yuna grins, "Thank you. Wait til you taste it though! You'll never want to drink anything else." Her perfect shoulder length black bob shines as she bends over to pour champagne into our plastic cups.

"Cheers girls! To eleventh grade next year and ...to a great summer for all of us!" says Yuna triumphantly placing the bottle on Sierra's nightstand and holding up her cup.

We bump our cups together and drink. "To us!"

THREE

Soon we're all taking photos with each other and new people start filing in. When Sierra's room gets so packed her desk lamp is knocked over, we move outside to the pool.

Within hours the entire yard and pool area is swarming with tenth grade graduates. Gaston, the best DJ in our class, has set up a sound system and is playing dance music mixing in voices of people we know saying funny things. Totally talented, we're dancing and intermittently laughing our heads off.

But when Sierra's Mom pops through to tell Sierra she is going to dinner with friends and she'll be back in a few hours, Gaston shifts gears. As soon as she backs the SUV out of the driveway, Gaston's music turns from super funny to super violent.

Woa, what happened? The energy shifts right away from light to dark and I look around to see if anyone else notices.

Boom. Boom. Boom.

"Slap that bitch up! Slap that bitch down! Put ah in her place an turn her around. Hoes stay down! Stay the fuck down! Blam Blam Blam! Ditty Blam. Nigga What!?" Gunfire, screams, and macabre music mixed in with curses fill Sierra's fenced in suburban yard.

My dance slows to a two-step and then stops. The next song is just as violent. I walk over to Sierra, "Woa, dude. I cannot listen to this. Can you ask him to play something else? Like that's non-violent please?"

"It's just a song," Sierra says. "Relax."

"Shoot the po-lice, kill the po-lice! Fuck the po-lice!" some rapper scream sings.

"I cannot listen to this, Sierra!!"

"Dude you are like so PG-13. Grow up!" yells Yuna who has apparently overheard my complaint a few bouncing heads over.

"But it's so violent! Listen to what they're saying."

"Ya but the beats are good. Just dance, don't listen to the lyrics," Sierra says steering me by the elbow further away from Yuna.

"How can I not listen to the lyrics?" I whine like a pup looking at the ground, tears hover in the corner of my eyes. "I should pack anyway," I say suddenly looking up at Sierra, a super fake smile on my face.

"Wait, you are leaving because of a song?" Sierra asks incredulous.

"Let the baby go home," sneers Yuna. "If she can't handle this, she shouldn't be here. Go back to kindergarten, Lena for God's sake. Remind me never to share champagne with her again."

Yuna narrows her black eyes at me, sniffs, tosses her shiny hair, and dancing over to Gaston, plants a kiss on his cheek. She whispers in his ear and points at me. Gaston smirks and nods, in on the secret.

"What is wrong with her? I wasn't even talking to her."

"It's okay Lena, she's right though. Gaston kinda has a reputation for starting out funny then going hard."

"But this is so violent and ... sad, how can you dance to it?"

"I don't know. I don't take things as personally as you, I guess. Just go home. You're fine." She hugs me. "Call me tomorrow."

I scan the crowd for Naia's strawberry blonde head and pink tiger stripes but don't see her. Then I grab my bag from Sierra's room and leave the party, pretending to talk on my phone to avoid further embarrassment.

———

AS SOON AS I am outside the gate, I allow the tears to fall freely. For a minute, I consider waiting on the porch and going back in later after Sierra's Mom comes home but forget that. I don't wanna hang out with people who think violence is entertaining. Even if I am PG-13, that's crazy! Why would anyone want to listen to or watch violence? Ugh, whatever, time for me to go.

I hoist my backpack over my shoulders and look up at the sky. It's pinky peach and purple with a little grey and gold mixed in. Dusk is my favorite time of day. I start walking the two miles from Sierra's house in Landfall to my house at Wrightsville Beach feeling deflated and sad about the music thing.

They are probably talking about me right now. "What a baby! Go back to kindergarten!" I hear Yuna saying in my mind's ear. But I'm not gonna pretend to be ok with violence. No way!

Popping my headphones on, I find the *Star Seed Nation* alert thing again and listen as I walk. "Signs of being a star seed include ... extreme sensitivity to and refusal to absorb violence in any form including entertainment and news."

Check.

"Caring immensely about the planet and all of life." Check.

"Possessing a sixth sense, having an ancestor with a sixth sense..."

Check. Check. My Grandma. Ok but like is any of that stuff real? Could there be an actual Galactic Council looking for people like me? I mean there are government organizations on Earth in every country so ... why couldn't there be?

My heart chakra turns from a slow sad, deflated spin to a happy, hopeful spin just thinking about it. I look up at the luminous pastel sky. Earth can be so beautiful and so ... weird.

FOUR

The next day Mom starts packing the car up early. The *She Speaks Talk Show* she's blaring in the driveway wakes me up.

"Today, 6 billion people live in areas plagued by water scarcity, with over two-thirds of the world's population living in water stressed regions. Scientists are searching for new ways to quench impending thirst."

"Mo-om! Do I have to come?" I ask walking up behind her in peach pajama bottom shorts and my 'just peachy' tee shirt. "Why can't I stay here and go to theatre camp or something useful this summer?"

"Lena, we've been over this," Mom says backing out and closing the shiny copper hatch, smudges of dirt on her red tank top and white shorts. Her light brown, grey streaked hair blows in a non-flattering angle with the ocean breeze as she moves forward to give me a hug.

I block it with exaggerated wonder woman arms and the wide legged stance I learned in self-defense class, my long braids whip around with the movement. I am just as tall as my mother now and much faster. It irritates her but I like her to know I'm not a little kid anymore and she shouldn't push me to do things I don't want.

I've been a straight A student for the past four years and that should count for something. If I'm not the one making direct decisions regarding my future, I should at least get a say!

"Mother be reasonable! Nobody wants to go this year but you! David doesn't wanna go and neither do I. It's gonna be weird up there without Gram! Why can't I just stay here with Dad and go to that two week theatre camp in Raleigh or... yoga camp in Charlotte?"

I look back at our house. The Sea Horse flag has already been raised. Mom does that to make it easy for renters to find. Houses in Wrightsville Beach rent for alot in summer.

Mom usually rents our house out June through August, and we spend the season in the mountains with my favorite person in the world, my Grandma. But Gram is dead now; so going to her house this year feels torturous and dumb- like clinging to a dying tradition- no pun intended.

Plus, it's not like we need the money. Mom just doesn't care what anyone wants but her. I know she already has her facial rejuvenation appointment prc-booked for September and that stuff costs a lot. All the Moms do it here. It's a status thing. If you have wrinkles you must be poor.

"Because Lena, it's what we always do." Mom says pushing her black cat eye sunglasses on top of her head, fixing her dark brown eyes on me, a slight edge in her voice.

Across the street an overweight pasty white couple in sun hats, pay the parking meter and begin unloading beach things from an SUV. Seagulls dive for french fries the lady spills from an over-full striped paper cup. Tourists.

Thwack. An ice cube hits me in the arm. Thwack. An ice cube hits me in the back. Thwack. An ice cube hits me on the cheek.

"That almost hit my eye, David!" I yell at my idiot brother. I am so not in the mood for him today.

David looks up from his cell phone and smirks. Playing a video game with one hand, his other hand holds a large plastic cup drained of sweet tea and full of ice. He tips the cup to his mouth, crosses his eyes in my direction, and spit launches another cube at me.

I dodge it. Pick it up, and throw the sand covered cube back at him. It hits him square in the chest. He takes a step towards me puffing himself up like a linebacker.

David doesn't want to go to the mountains either. He wants to stay here and surf all summer but Mom is not budging.

"Mom! David is spitting ice at me!"

"Don't antagonize your sister!" Mom says loudly giving David the stink eye. "Aaannnd you know the rules about plastic, young man. We are a zero-waste family for a reason. So why in the world do you have a plastic cup in your hand?"

"Sorry. Dad bought it for me."

Mom freezes and anger washes over her face. Whether to use or not use plastic is an epic battle between my mother and father. Mom tries hard to be zero waste and Dad doesn't give a ship.

"For someone who enjoys the ocean as much as you do, I hope you would be a little more conscious about using reusable containers, young man. Did y'all see the trash that washed up on the beach this morning?"

"Yea," David scowls, "I pulled two plastic bottles out the ocean this mornin' when me and Dad were surfin'. He pulled out three."

"And what did you do with them?"

"Put them next to the trashcan because it was full."

"Thank you, that is exactly my point. When you pick plastic up and throw it away, it still has to go somewhere. The best way to reduce plastic is to *never buy it*. When you buy plastic you create the *need* for it. Does that make sense?"

"I know, Mom. I'm sorry. I'll reuse the cup." He stares down at his tan, sandy feet and sighs.

You rarely win with Mom. She is like a mountain, very hard to move. Once in awhile you get a win though, so David and I do our due diligence. Tag teamwork to wear her down has always yielded the best results. Dad is usually working so he's no help either way. He just cares about money, which Mom probably married him for, they have nothing else in common.

"Mom!" I launch into a final attempt, the knot in my stomach starting to feel more like a fire, "If David and I stay here with Dad", I pause searching for the right words, "you would get *so* much more work done on your book! You'd have the whole house to yourself. You ...you could write like 24-7!"

"Lena!" Mom bends forward at the waist like a chicken about to peck grain, "You and David are coming with me."

"But it doesn't make sense!" I squeal throwing my hands in the air and bouncing on my toes for emphasis. "David is practically an adult!"

"Seventeen is not practically an adult these days and y'all are not staying with your father while he's working on that chem- ical case. He's in DC nearly every week now and those protestors..." Mom's eyes turn moist then darken and she pulls her sunglasses down. "Those protestors ...I wouldn't be surprised if they turn violent one of these days."

David laughs, "They have nothing better to do, right?"

"How does that even resemble funny, David?" I turn on my heel and stare my brother down, hands clenched in tight fists.

"It's funny to me. Remember that time the news covered Dad squirting the protestors with vinegar in that water gun because they were blocking his office?"

"Yeah..."

"And one of them was Mrs. Powell, Jules Mom?"

I nod but don't say anything. I remember because the next day at school Jules told everyone that whenever someone got cancer in Wilmington it was my father's fault. Then a picture of an ugly, deformed fetus mysteriously appeared on my locker with the words, "Cancer Causer!" in black sharpie and every time I took it down someone put it back up. That lasted an entire week. I think I cried for a month.

My father is a lawyer. He defends bad guys, like huge anti-environment corporations for a living and gets paid a lot of money to do it. His big client around here is Chemican, a company that's been dumping Gen Z, a toxic chemical into the Cape Fear River, Wilmington's drinking water, for like half a century. Gen-Z has been linked to all types of cancer and other diseases.

You can't get into his office without walking past a dozen people holding signs that say things like, "Bad Men Work Here," "My Eight-Year-Old Has Cancer," "Protect our Water, Protect our Kids," and "Chemican is Evil."

David laughs again. He literally has no brain.

When another ice cube hits me in the forehead, the knot in my stomach bursts into flames and I need to get away before I kill him.

"This family is so dysfunctional!" I yell. "My brother is a freaking idiot, my parents only care about money, and the one person who ever really got me is dead. How am I supposed to do anything good in life?!" I end like I'm on stage closing a scene, turning one complete circle hands outstretched palms to the sky, eyes wide, waiting for someone to offer something...some morsel of hope.

My mother claps slowly one clap at a time squinting in the morning sun. "See, you don't need to go to theatre camp, you're already a professional actress!"

David gunshot guffaws a "Ha!" and his sandy blonde head

shoots back like someone socked him one. "Ya and you totally put the D in dysfunctional, dork. That was great... can you do it again?"

He grabs a handful of ice and launches it high in the air above my head. Ice cubes rain on me bouncing once on the ground before melting at my feet. One or two plunk me on the head on the way down.

David continues to laugh but his eyes tell me he's just as upset as I am. "But you're right, I don't wanna go to the mountains. I wanna stay here and surf with my buds."

"Son," Mom says slow and low trying to stay calm, "you failed eleventh grade *because s*urfing and your buds are a *major* distraction. *You* are going to be studying in the mountains all summer far away from your friends, so you pass your exam and graduate on time."

"And Lena," Mom says turning to me, "my daughter who I love, my straight A student... I *know* you're upset but let's make the best of it, ok? Attitude is half the battle. We'll have fun up there. We'll go shopping, swimming in the lake, I'll finish my book... and maybe... by the end of summer the Chemican case will close and we won't have to worry about protestors anymore."

She turns to me pouting; her ruby earrings catch a ray of sun. Those earrings were my grandmother's and it's just enough to put me right over the edge. If anyone says another word to me I will scream or cry or both.

I run past my brother punching him in the shoulder on the way back into the house. I hear Mom say, "Teen girls are dealing with a lot of hormones, David," as I run up the stairs to my room. "Try to be nicer to your sister, please."

I put my headphones on loud, pull my black out shades down, and lock my door. I throw myself on *my* bed in *my* room that I don't want strangers sleeping in all summer!

FIVE

A few hours later, I wake up to a loud crash. The light is dim like it's almost night. High winds howl around the sides of our house. I scurry over to the window and rub my eyes. Trashcans blow down the street, banging into mailboxes, cars, and houses. Torrential rain pummels the street. Trees are blowing sideways.

What is going on? How long did I sleep and why didn't anyone wake me? My cell phone vibrates on the bed. I must have turned the sound off.

The text says, "Coastal Carolinas Evacuate. Hurricane Ivanka. Level four Hurricane. Evacuate. Evacuate."

What? It's too early in the season for a hurricane. Plus, we weren't warned!

I tap mom's number and get, "The cell phone you dialed is not in service." Dad's number gives me the same message and so does David's. I try Naia and Sierra, same thing!

Oh my gosh! Am I alone? Where the fuck is everybody? I grab my half-packed backpack and throw in headphones, laptop,

cell phone charger, my favorite sweatshirt and the Lemurian seed crystal and selenite wand Gram gave me for my 13th birthday. I have no idea what I'm gonna do!

"Mo-om?! David?! Where are you?"

I run to the back door. Tree branches wave frantically scratching the windows. The awful scraping noise gets louder when I open the back door and lean out. The wind swings the door open hard and hits the side of the house.

"Mom? David? Dad?" I shout into the wind. Did they really leave without me?

Maybe something happened? Are they mad at me for yelling?

Struggling against a churning, angry wind, I have to throw my full weight against the door to get it closed. I lock it behind me and run to Mom's room still searching even though I can feel and know I am alone. More crashes from outside. I look down at the street from Mom's bedroom. The seahorse flag is whipping maniacally in the churning air.

Goosebumps stand up on my arms and legs and the back of my neck. I have no fucking idea what to do!

Headlights in the distance... Is that Dad's truck? Dad's truck!!

Dad's truck is pulling up to the front of our house!

I run downstairs. The door flies open. Dad stands there like some movie hero soaked and bewildered. His long sleeve blue dress shirt clings to his arms and chest and his funny peach tie with beach umbrellas flaps wildly around his head.

Behind him a dark sky swirls with fast moving menacing clouds and thick bolts of lightening. Thunder booms so close!

"Lena!" my father yells, "We need to get out of here now. "Where are Mom and David?"

"Halfway to the mountains by now!" Dad yells above thunder and wind.

"Why did they leave without me?" "Talk on the way, babe! Let's go...now!"

Wind stronger than a hundred hands pushes me as Dad and I run to the truck. I almost lose my balance but Dad grabs my arm and pulls me toward the truck. A bike somersaults down the street and a skateboard slides behind it like a ghost rider.

Eyes worried and squinting, Dad holds the truck door open for me to jump in. The rain is so loud even in Dad's cushy, sound proof executive truck I hardly hear him yell, "Seatbelt!"

Driving over our yard, the tires make a circle in our perfect green grass and I imagine Mom scolding him but there is no time for that because, bam! That nice little tree the landscapers just planted in Ms. Piel's front yard uproots in front of our eyes and flies down the street landing on the back of a shiny new BMW crashing out the back window.

"Oh my gosh, Dad! What *is h*appening?"

"It's Hurricane Ivanka. Came without warning. Looked tiny out at sea on the news this morning. Was supposed to dissipate, turn into a summer storm. It's too early in the season for a hurricane like this..."

Up ahead, by the Wrightsville Beach Bridge, a police officer standing next to his patrol car waves frantically. The rain has saturated his uniform. He looks like a drowned rat. Water drips from his mustache and plunks off his hat. Officer Delaney. He's usually all spiffed up with a waxy handlebar mustache.

Dad rolls the window down.

"Y'all should have evacuated hours ago. You're really pushing it, Linnigan. Didja see anyone else back there?" he asks jerking his head and a hooked thumb across the bridge towards the island.

My father is a pretty big fish in a small pond, everyone knows him here. They're either for or against him. The Police here like him because he sends a big donation every Christmas.

"No, just us. No one else on the road," Dad says.

Rain pours into the truck sideways. Officer Delaney looks scared. Rain cascades off his drooping waxy mustache, which twitches nervously. He steps backwards towards the police car.

"Well then get goin' inland to high ground as fast as you can Linnigan an' good luck."

"Thanks, Delaney. Good luck to you too."

Lightening lights up the sky slicing it in two, illuminating massive storm clouds rolling like a dirty freight train towards the ocean. Thunder booms so loud and close I let out a scream. A shopping cart smashes into the side of the truck on my side. I start to shake.

"We've got the perfect vehicle for a hurricane, babe," Dad says trying to calm me down. "This truck weighs over a ton and is nearly impossible to flip."

"Nearly impossible, Dad?"

My father swerves as the trunk of a car rips off and flies out in front of us. He pushes the 4wheel drive button and we head towards the highway slow, chaos billowing around us like some crazy movie. Dad's smart watch lights up with Mom's face.

"Did you get her, David? Is she safe?"

He presses a button on the steering wheel. Mom's voice transfers to the truck audio system. The sound of crying fills the interior.

"Hi Mom," I squeak. "We're okay so far. Why did you leave without me?"

"Honey, I am so sorry! I thought I would let you stay one more day. Your father was, uh huh huh (crying) was going to take you and your friends to a movie and dinner tonight and...and drive you to the mountains tomorrow. Uh huh huh..."

Dad swerves to the right super-fast. My head hits the window. A traffic light crashes to the street behind us. Rain is coming down so hard and the wind is bending trees like licorice straws.

"Doreen!" Dad yells. You'll have to talk to her later! I need to concentrate!"

Dad turns the audio off and Mom's crying vanishes. The silence in the truck is as thick as the rain is heavy. Another traffic light up ahead blinks red and Dad drives right past it onto the highway. Chest heaving, his strong arms grip the steering wheel.

"Ok. We made it to the highway. We should be fine now. We go slow and steady and we'll be fine..."

There is hardly anyone else on the road; only a few semi-trucks and cars driving real slow. We pass them one by one. I look over at a lady driving. She does not look back only straight ahead with this terrified expression on her face.

I try to swallow but can't. My mouth is so dry.

Rummaging in my backpack, I find my Lemurian seed crystal and hold it tightly in my hand, stroking the triangular indents with my thumb.

The wind keeps pushing us to the right and dad keeps adjusting. A shoe bouncing off the front windshield gets stuck on our wiper blade and goes back and forth making an awful squeal as the rubber sticks to the glass. A shoe?

"God damn shit storm from Hades!" Dad yells. "Just what we need! Just what we fucking need!"

He pulls over and gets out, removing the shoe with a string of harsh curses. I know Dad is scared too because he never curses around me. I hold my crystal and pray.

Please let us live. Please let us live I beg squeezing my eyes closed. Suddenly an intense violet hue washes over the blackness behind my eyes.

"Earth is purifying. Do not be afraid. You will not be hurt." I hear my dead Grandmother's voice in my head and for one second I smell her warm cinnamon rose scent.

Surprised, I sit up straight still keeping my eyes closed and see Gram's face clearly. I see her green eyes, a shade darker than mine, her fluffy white hair, long neck and pretty hands and nails.

I see the pearl ring she wore on her pinky and the seashell necklace I made for her when I was five.

Dad gets back in slamming the door and grumbling.

"Gram, I am trying not to cry or be afraid," I tell her in my mind.
"Sing."

I start to sing whatever comes to mind. I sing "somewhere over the rainbow, "these are a few of my favorite things," "the national anthem," and Christmas songs. Whatever I can remember, I sing.

I sing and I sing while the rain comes down in sheets. The stressed angry look on Dad's face softens. My singing calms us and we get thirty or so miles down. By then the ditches on the side of the highway begin to overflow and the muddy water swirls around us. Even in Dad's big 4wheel drive truck it reaches the middle of the tires. Dad's driving slows to a crawl and then a stop when a semi-truck lying on its side blocks the only part of the highway not flooded.

We are stuck.

"Fucking shit!" Dad yells. "Shit, shit, shit!"

"Dad?" I whisper.

He looks over at me, "I am sorry, Lena, I should have come home earlier. I was working on a case and I didn't think the storm would amount to anything..."

Shaking his head he pounds the steering wheel then blows out a long huffing breath.

"We'll have to wait here until the rain stops."

"What?!"

"There's no way around this truck."

I watch horrified as my normally calm in control father pushes the roadside emergency button with a shaky finger.

A woman's scratchy smoker's voice blares into the interior of the truck, "Emergency Roadside Assistance. Are you in a life-threating situation?"

"I am on the side of I-40 with my teenage daughter in a flood. There's a semi-truck on its side blocking the road. We can't get around it."

"We have someone on the way to service the truck, sir. In this weather, it will take a few hours. Please be patient and stay where you are. Do not attempt anything heroic."

My father snorts at this, "Thank you. Please get here as fast as you can."

"Yes, sir. Hold tight. We'll be there as fast as we can."

So my father and I do the only thing we can do. Wait. We wait while the rain pelts the truck from all directions and watch. We watch as the water rises to the middle of the tires then to the bottom of the door and keeps going. Four hours pass and I need to pee. I don't say anything though I just hold it and pray that someone comes soon. I wonder if the driver in that truck is dead.

Finally, after what seems like an eternity, the roadside emergency army tanker comes and pulls the truck over just enough to let us pass. Water gushes around it and dad does not wait for instructions. He starts the engine back up and we drive right around that thing towards the mountains in door deep muddy water. I've never really liked Dad's truck but for sure, if we were in a car or anything lower to the ground, we would have drowned waiting.

The driving is slow and the rain is still fast but we make good time now. Dad is determined to get us to the mountains tonight. Finally, about an hour past Charlotte, the wind and rain slow to a summer storm and a little bit of blue peeps out around the grey clouds. Dad pulls over to get gas. I hop out and stretch under the awning tired, hungry, and shaking with adrenaline.

"I need to eat. I haven't eaten since breakfast and it's almost nine," Dad says inserting his card into the gas pump.

"I'm hungry too," I say in a wilted, wavering voice.

Behind the gas station in the corner of the parking lot is a Mrs. Mindy's Diner. The handwritten sign out front says, "Home Cookin' at its finest. Today's specials: Chicken and dumplings. Shrimp and Grits. Cheeseburger and Fries. Chicken Caesar Salad. Best milkshakes in Carolina."

Dad nods towards the diner. "Let's go there."

SIX

Everything in Mrs. Mindy's Diner is shiny metallic blue and silver. Dad and I slide into a booth, the waitress walks over and smiles. She is tall and skinny, around Mom's age with huge boobs, probably fake, and too much perfume, something really flowery. I cough once and cover my nose with my hand trying to give her the hint without being rude.

"Hi, Mrs. Mindy," Dad says.

"Well, aren't you funny!" Booberella laughs at my Dad's corny joke placing a hand on her heart and tilting her hips back so her butt sticks up. "Y'all are scapin' the hoorrycayn I 'spect?" she asks with a deep southern accent eyes wandering over our wet clothes.

"Yes and we barely made it," Dad says shooting her his best bill-board smile. We've been on the road all day. We're starving but happy to be alive right, kiddo?"

"Dad! Can you not call me that in public?! I'm fifteen! But yeah," I soften, "We're alive and hungry." I smile sheepishly over the shiny laminated menu.

"Well ah for one am glad y'all are alahv, shoogs. Now what are ya'll havin'?" she asks batting clumpy black eyelashes at my father and not, for one second, looking at me.

"Steak medium rare, mashed potatoes, green beans and a side salad," Dad says without looking at the menu. "And a sweet tea."

"Um, Ill have a chicken Caesar salad and a bottle of water, please."

"Sorry, sweets. We're plum outta bottled water," skinny big boobs says twirling a ribbon of bleached hair staring at Dad and sticking out her boobs and butt again. A lot of women flirt with my father right in front of me. It's weird.

"Out of bottled water?" Dad asks.

"Yassir, we had a run on it today. A dozen or so people from Wilmington came up here just like y'all and bought us out... something about a chemical spill on accounta the hooricayne an hah winds."

"Really?" Dad asks knitting his brows together. Then turning to me, thumps his hands on the table so hard the silver- ware jumps. His whole face has changed. He's got that look in his eye like when he is about to turn a major deal. I call it the money look.

"This is the sign I've been waiting for, kiddo. You're Uncle's been asking me to invest with him. He's got a hot one on the line again. Order your food and I'll tell you what I mean." He nods sideways at the waitress like he doesn't want her to hear his big idea.

Uncle Leo, my Dad's older half-brother, is a commercial producer in Los Angeles with a sixth sense for investments

that's made him so wealthy he owns an island. Every year he sends me a birthday card with a check and an open casting call invitation addressed to: "Our Rising Star," because I take the lead in school plays. I haven't gone to one yet but I'd like to.

"What?" I stare at Dad then back at the waitress. "There's no bottled water?"

"No bottled water, shoogs."

"Uh, then I'll have um a sweat tea too," I say passing the menu back to Booberella. "Did you happen to hear where the chemical spill was?" I gulp.

"Wilmington, shoogs and I heard there was an oil spill too. Bad day for North Carolina."

My hands fly up to cover my mouth.

"Is that where y'all are from?" she asks arching one skinny penciled in eyebrow.

I nod, hands still over my mouth.

My father pulls out his phone to check the waitress' facts.

Booberella and I watch his face reading and wait.

"She's right," he confirms looking at me over his reading glasses. "There were both oil *and* chemical spills in Wilmington today caused by that goddamn bitch of a hurricane."

"I'm sorry, sweets," says Booberella to me collecting the menus. "I hate to be the bearer of bad news." She touches my hand lightly, consoling before walking away hips swishing back and forth towards the kitchen.

Dad folds his hands and tilts his head, "So now we know.

Guess what we're going to do?" "Help with the clean up?"

My father shakes his head, "Drumroll please and I'll tell you."

"Dad just tell me..."

"Drumroll?"

"Ughhhhh! Fine!" I drumroll on the table with cupped hands.

"Louder, please."

"Dad!" I kick him under the table.

"Oww!" He laughs trapping my kicking foot under the table with his legs then releasing it. "You gave me better drum rolls when you were five. I miss those drum rolls."

"I'm losing interest..." I glower pulling out my cell phone. "Ok, ok! Put that away!" Dad says practically giddy leaning

across the table cupping my hand in his like he's about to propose or something. "Your Uncle Leo's got a brilliant new investment on the line and I have a feeling it is *the one*... the one that will buy me that island next to his."

"What does that have to do with running out of bottled water *and or* the oil and chemical spills?" I ask pulling my hand away. "Which by the way was probably your client..."

Dad ignores my question. "The investment... is a water substitute called Wüter," he says simply flourishing his hands for effect.

"A water *substitute*?"

"Follow the golden thread here, babe," Dad winks at me. I hate it when he calls me babe.

"How much do you think it costs to clean up an average sized chemical spill?"

"I have no idea, Dad."

"It costs millions of dollars to clean up a minor spill... a *minor* spill and billions to clean up a large one. So what usually happens is the company responsible does as little as possible to pass EPA inspection. The water quality suffers and continues to get worse. But let's sidestep that for a minute," Dad presses the pads of his fingers together and taps them to his forehead.

He closes his cool blue eyes seeming to be in deep thought. When he opens them again, the problem solver concerned look is replaced by the money gleam. His eyes flicker a fraction of a second looking momentarily reptilian, ice cold and very far away.

"If Chemican *is* responsible for the spill which to be honest, I think you're right, then I know the volume of the container that spilled. It is a large volume and highly hazardous. So if in fact it was the container that dumped into the Cape Fear River, Wilmington will not have access to local drinking water for *a long time*. That's one company that doesn't give a shit about pure water, I'll tell you that right now."

"Omygosh Dad, why do you work for them then? That is evil."

"I don't work *for* them, they commission me. I work for myself and for my family. Just follow along here while I make this next point, mmkay?"

"But..."

"Babe, just follow along," my father says sternly. "Ok," I acquiescence softly suddenly trying not to cry.

"The oil spill not the chemical spill will get cleaned up first... to keep tourist money coming in. Wilmington needs a clean ocean but it will take a long time and probably never be the same."

My father and I lock eyes. I'm about to protest but he silences me with a hand gesture.

"Let me finish. Back to the Cape Fear River," he pauses rubbing the back of his neck and looking out the window. "That river has been too polluted to use for drinking water for decades. Even before you were born, it was polluted. That's why we use a whole house water filter system. So if the *entire* Gen-Z chemical container fell in, Wilmington won't be able to use that water anymore... not even filtering the shit out of it. Ok? Still with me?"

I nod.

"When water is too polluted to drink, *people are thirsty*. Hell, people are thirsty now. Nearly seventy percent of the world lives with water scarcity on a daily basis... and it ain't gettin' better. This is where *we* come in with our water substitute."

Skinny Big Boobs sets sweet teas, spoons, and straws in front of us interrupting our conversation with a clang. She wags her finger at my father. "I know why you look so familiar! I seen yer face on that billboard on the way to the beach! Hey, Carla, we got a famous lawyer in here!"

My father and his law firm partner, Frank Mackey, advertise on a billboard on I-40, smiling over the highway for the world to see. The sign says, "Linnigan and Mackey. We Fight for Big Business." Millions of people recognize him because of that sign. It annoys me but I know he loves it.

The Leo astrology sign loves attention. My father is a Leo sun, Leo moon *and* a Leo rising. That is a lot of Leo and a lot of attention.

"Excuse me," I say. "I need to use the restroom."

Walking as fast as I can to the ladies room, the last thing I see before the door closes, is every waitress in the place swarming over my father like bees on a hive. My father is sucking it up with a straw.

"Omygosh," I say staring into the mirror. "If these are the

changes Kiki Astromatrix predicted, please let them get better. Please."

My hand shakes as I turn the faucet to wash my hands and face with cool water. "I am grateful for this water," I hear myself say. "I love this water." Then I go into a stall, shut the door, close my eyes and breathe.

SEVEN

By the time we pull into the gravel driveway at Daffodil House it's close to midnight. Daffodil House is my grandmom's big yellow house in the mountains. Well, it was Gram's house. When she died she left it to Mom. So, now it's ours, or Mom's, I guess.

Whoever owns it, the big yellow house in the mountains is called Daffodil House because Pop, Mom's Dad, painted it the color of Mom's favorite flower for her ninth birthday. Mom has told me that story so many times I could tell it in my sleep.

I used to love being at Daffodil House when Gram was alive. Gram and I could and would have entire conversations without opening our mouths. She was the *only* person in the world I could do that with. She was the only person in my entire family I felt truly connected with. Besides that, her house always smelled good, like ginger and cinnamon cookies, roses, beeswax candles, pottery, paint, and eucalyptus at once.

I don't know how I feel about being here now. It's the first time I've been here since she passed. But she contacted me today or maybe that was just my imagination because I thought I might die in the hurricane.

My head and heart pound with overwhelm as I climb out of the truck and stretch my arms high, inhaling fresh mountain air. Lightening bugs flash against an indigo sky popping with silver stars. The mountains I've loved since I was a baby welcome me and I breath a deep sigh of relief to just... be alive.

The front yard motion detector light flicks on, and Daffodil

House illumined, looks just as I remember. The green lawn is

perfectly manicured and so are the rose bushes. Roses all

different colors, from deep red to light pink, white, yellow, and orange, surround the house. The porch swing sways in the warm summer breeze. A grey cat with a white patch on its chest, startled by the light, jumps off the porch and slinks off into the night.

The door bangs open and Mom runs over with a wine glass in her hand, smothering me in her chest with her free arm. David follows a few paces behind, shirtless, hair up in a loose man bun.

"Honey, I am so sorry...I thought I was doing the right thing letting you stay one more night." Mom's white wine splashes on my arm as she sob shakes so happy to see us.

Dad takes Mom's glass and finishes the wine handing her back the empty glass.

"I hope there's more Doreen, we've had a long day and I need to unwind." He hugs Mom and me together then claps David on the shoulder and pulls him in too. "What a storm, buddy. Traffic lights blowing down, trucks flipping over!"

"Glad you guys are ok," David says ruffling my hair. He extracts himself from the hug. "We saw uh Mom and I saw ... on the news that Chemican's toxic waste storage tank thing or whatever fell into the river *and* an oil tank spilled like off the coast of Wrightsville Beach. Dude, can that be true? In one storm? Did you hear?"

Panic blossoms in my belly like sprouts on a bean and my head pounds. Sometimes when I'm super anxious my spirit tries to float out of my body which makes me even more anxious because... what if I don't catch it in time and can't get back in?

Breathe Lena. Breathe. Stay in the now.

I look down at my feet. They are in the right place, beneath me, on the ground. The gold sandals and peach toenails are definitely mine.

But everyone's voice is getting farther and farther away.

Will I even have a future if there is no clean water? Will drinking a water substitute make us less human?

What will the world be like when I'm my parent's age? Will humans be extinct by then?

Air is pressing in on me. Pressing down on me. My breath becomes shallow. I begin to float... I look at my hands. At the amethyst ring and bracelet I put on this morning that seems like a year ago. Anxiety is winning. I am spinning out.

A heavy-handed thump on the back, knocks me back into the now.

"Earth to Lena. Come in, Lena." David cups his hands like a megaphone booming his scratchy, nasal voice in my ear. "We are waiting for you on Earth. Come back to the mother ship."

I straighten up, rigid, back in my body. Mixed emotions of gratitude and irritation land like fat snowflakes melting on my hot cheeks. I swear sometimes I don't know whether to hug or hit my idiot brother.

My voice must be straggling on another planet though because I can't find it to speak the, "hey!" I was going for. What comes out instead is like a slow leak of air from a slashed tire, "Hhhhhhaaaa."

Meeting David's eyes briefly, I see he meant to be helpful not hurtful in his own strange way. He puts his arm around me and I lean my head on his shoulder. Somehow he still smells like warm sun and ocean air. Slumping into him for support, I walk into my dead grandmother's house with my flawed family, my weirdo brother and my even weirder parents, one foot in front of the other.

EIGHT

An hour later, I am drinking my second cup of peppermint tea, lying in bed in the messy old lilac room, which used to be Mom's. I haven't cleaned or unpacked a thing. My sheets haven't been washed and I'm probably sitting on top of a year's worth of dust.

The clock says 1:11AM. Usually when I check the time and see the same number like 3:33, or 4:44, or 11:11 it makes me feel good, like I am on the right track or something. But when I see 1:11 tonight I just feel doomed. Worrying thoughts bombard me like video game gun spray.

Pew pew pew.

Did my friends make it out of the hurricane? Sierra and Naia never texted me back.

How bad is the oil spill?

How bad is the chemical spill?

Will Dad keep defending evil Chemican?

What happens if we run out of water? What will the substitute taste like?

How did it get this bad?

Sleep is not coming anytime soon so what should I do? I could lie here all night worrying and maybe die of a heart attack by morning. I can read. I can watch something on Netflix or...I can research.

Research sounds the most promising and I did pack chocolate... Chocolate makes the idea tempting enough for me to actually move.

A minute later, I am back in bed with my laptop, cell phone, and the first piece of a fair-trade sea salt caramel milk chocolate bar melting in my mouth.

I first text Sierra and Naia: *Where are you guys? Did you make it out of the hurricane?*

Then I type, "chemical + oil spill + water + North Carolina." A lot comes up. I read the first story:

"Earlier today, Hurricane Ivanka ravaged the Coastal Carolinas causing billions of dollars in damage with a death toll of twelve and counting. Hurricane Ivanka will go on record as the hardest hitting hurricane to hit the Carolinas since Hurricane Fran in 1996.

Record breaking high winds, heavy rains, and flooding did more than damage property here. Early this afternoon, winds up to 150 miles per hour knocked a power line into a large Chemican storage tower exploding a high volume of concentrated toxins into the Cape Fear River, the local drinking water supply.

Water from the Cape Fear River is deemed unsafe to drink until further notice. Water Usage Restrictions have been bumped from a level two to a level five state-wide in both North and South Carolina.

If you do not yet have a water meter in your home or office, call the number below to have one installed. Meters must be installed by June 15th when fines will begin. Residents are advised to not drink the water in New Hanover County. Water may be used for laundry, dish washing, and short showers only."

I flip to the next story and click on a video. A tan blonde woman with a shining gold cross pendant is walking alongside the ocean at Wrightsville Beach.

"More major hurricane damage. A loose boat rammed into an oil tank a mile off the coast of Wilmington, North Carolina, spilling a large volume of oil into the ocean. Beaches are closed until further notice.

Cleanup crews are working on salvaging what wildlife they can. Volunteers are welcome and encouraged, please sign up at your local courthouse."

I watch with horror and disbelief as the camera pans over Wrightsville Beach. The ocean is black. Oily black fish and other sea creatures too covered in gunk and debris to tell what they are flop around on the beach gasping, most in piles of dead already. A dozen people in hazmat suits are trying to clean off oil coated dolphins and seagulls covered in black gunk hop around too heavy to fly.

The camera pans over the houses closest to the beach. Windows are knocked out, one roof is torn off, cars and trucks are flipped over, and the normally well-manicured streets are in total shambles.

We were in that hurricane. Shit, I can hardly believe my eyes.

A real-life nightmare and my father is making money off it defending those greedy corporations.

Dad's face floats into my mind, "Drum roll, please...Your Uncle Leo's got a hot new investment on the line. A water substitute called Wüter..."

But if there is no clean water, how will we live? And if we do live, how gross will life be without clean water?

I close my laptop, heart thumping out of my chest. I twist the cap off the lavender essential oil I always keep in my back- pack, drop a few drops in my hands and breathe deeply several times. I put two pillows under my knees and place my Lemurian seed crystal over my heart. As comfortable as I can physically get, I put my blackout mask on and pray for sleep.

"LENA! I am so happy you're here! I've missed you so much, sweetheart!" Gram's hale figure dressed in a dark green pants suit and slim gold belt, bends over me, gold and silver light bursting around her like moon and sunray as she kisses me on the cheek. A loose strand of soft white hair, done up in braids, tickles my cheek.

"I missed you too, Gram."

"This is the summer of transition for you Lena Lenora." Her eyes and face crinkle with love as she speaks and she looks so beautiful. The most beautiful woman in the world, I think.

I nod and smile somehow knowing what she means but not fully understanding. There's kind of a difference. You know something with your body and heart and understand with your mind.

Gram takes two steps back and holds out her hand to me. I glide out of bed to take it and we walk to the open window, jump lightly and fly into the air together, flying over Daffodil House, toward Black Mountain. Tiny silver stars pop out one by one by one against an inky indigo sky. The dark mountain, outlined in magenta light, looks ominously beautiful.

We fly close to the mountain, skimming the tops of trees with our bare feet. The air is clear and warm. Gram shows me an open field and points out a circle made of stones. Behind it stands a cave with a hazy crystalline light flickering from deep within.

I want to stop and visit but we fly past it to the top of the mountain. The ocean is visible from here. Black and brown oil swirls lapping the sandy shore. Dead bodies line the beach, birds, sea creatures, and humans. The scent of oil and death punch me like an icy fist hard in the stomach. I inhale sharply, afraid and squeeze Gram's hand.

On the other side of the mountain the polluted ocean is no longer visible. A happier landscape with a full moon illuminating waterfalls, rivers, and a big blue lake, greets us. A dozen or so people roasting s'mores and drinking beer over a bonfire on the shore of the lake wave to us like it is no big deal we are flying. Bonfire rages up as we pass and the wind blows spreading the hungry flames. The partiers scream trying to tamp out the fire beginning to digest everything in its path.

A flock of wild geese flying in beautiful formations approach us. As they grow closer their pretty black bird eyes change to fiery, demonic red eyes. They weave around us, angry honks mingling with human screams. One of their wings brushes my arm. A dark oily stain burns my skin and I cry out in pain brushing it off with my free hand.

Warm rain begins to fall soothing my burned arm, the geese's fiery red eyes turn back to black. Suddenly, I am no longer a girl holding onto her grandmother's hand. I am a goose flying in the gaggle.

The bird nearest me transmits a message, *"Ritual. Ritual is the key to unlock your birth gifts and activate your invitation. You must welcome the elements as Earth's messengers and friends with ritual. Your Rite of Passage has begun."*

Woooshhh. I return through my bedroom window and land back in my body with a thump.

NINE

I open an eye and turn to look at the clock. 4:44AM. My heart is pounding in my ears and my nightshirt is soaked with sweat. Omigosh, I need to write that dream down! I sit up rubbing my eyes trying to remember exactly what was said.

But still so exhausted from yesterday, I cannot move to put my feet on the floor yet. My heart slows and I lie back down and close my eyes. I turn on my side, readjusting the pillow between my knees and one under my arm. The physical need to sleep longer eases my breathing into a rhythm and I snuggle deeper into the pillows.

When I wake up again, I am dry and well rested. Bright sunlight slicing through the blinds tells me it's past nine. I yawn and stretch, kicking off dusty shooting star print sheets. The dream resurfaces like my reflection in a pond, wavy but consistent. I scurry over to my backpack to grab my notebook and pen.

Just as I write down, "welcome the elements as Earth's messengers and friends..." the doorbell rings.

Sitting in bed cross-legged, pen poised, I press my ear against the wall to listen. I can vaguely make out a girl and mom talking. Probably some kid trying to sell something. But intuition tells me this is inaccurate. This person has something to do with me.

Underneath "welcome Earth's messengers" my hand writes, "water must be protected," of its own accord.

Jumping up, I throw the door open, run down the hall to Gram's room which I guess is Mom's now, and look out the window.

From here you can see the entire yard and walkway to the front door. A medium sized grey dog with floppy ears and an orange collar is sniffing the grass. I stay where I am and watch, hunched over, hair in messy braids with sleep sand still in my eyes.

A minute passes and I hear the door close.

Then I see a girl around my age with curly, dark brown hair stroll down the front walk. It's the kind of hair that if you stick a pencil in it, will stay there all day. The girl is wearing jean shorts and a lime green tank top, the color of tree frogs. Her feet are bare. In one hand she holds a leash, in the other hand a pair of black leather flip-flops, which she tosses on the ground and steps into.

The girl turns around and looks up at me. She waves and I duck away. I would rather not meet someone in sweaty nightclothes.

I run back down the hall to the bathroom; wash my face and brush my teeth and hair. I put moisturizer on with SPF that has lavender, chamomile, and calendula in it and smells divine. It's for combination skin, which I have.

I smile in the mirror and say, "Hi, I am Lena. Nice to meet you."

Then I run to my room to get dressed.

I pull on jean shorts and my favorite purple tank top. Purple always makes my eyes look super green and I like that. I put in my amethyst earrings and slip on the matching bracelet. Finally, I pull my long hair into a ponytail and run downstairs.

Mom calls to me from the kitchen. "Lena, I made breakfast!" "Who was at the door?" I ask heading in that direction.

Mom comes out of the kitchen and stands in the dining room. Her hair is in a bun and she is holding a "Best Dad in the World" coffee mug.

"A girl was looking for her dog. It was the cutest thing. She knocked on the door to ask if I'd seen him then the dog walks right up behind her wagging his tail." Mom sips her coffee. "Nice looking dog, too. Grey, a Weimaraner I think."

"Is she our neighbor? Which way did she go?" I ask leaning out the front door, scanning the street.

"Come and eat first. It's Sunday. I made breakfast."

Realizing I have no way to know which way the girl and her dog went or where they live, I close the door and join Mom in the kitchen. I sit down and Mom pours me freshly squeezed grape-fruit juice. It is my absolute favorite. I drink it in one long gulp.

"Thanks, Mom. What else did the girl say? Do you know who she is and where she lives? Do you think she's my age?" I fire questions at Mom like an Aries rising while she serves me a vegetable omelet, crisp bacon and a piece of toast with butter and strawberry jam on one side.

"I didn't think to ask any of that but..." Mom begins.

"Jees, you really went all out this morning," I interrupt popping a piece of perfectly crisp bacon in my mouth.

Mom looks pleased.

"Your Uncle Leo is flying in from Los Angeles today. Dad went to pick him up at the airport. They'll have a business lunch then come here. They have a proposition for you."

"For me?"'

"For you," Mom affirms raising her eyebrows over the coffee mug. "But it is Sunday, family day sooo would you like to go to the lake before they get here? Maybe your brother will come too. Whaddya think?"

She folds her hands on the table and watches me eat with satisfaction.

The bacon is perfect. Crispy and crunchy with no grease, just the way I like it. No flop at all.

Yum.

Mom is funny, she makes a great breakfast but when it comes to dinner, she can get a little lost.

I forget about the girl and her dog for a moment. "Okay. The lake sounds good. You want me to wake David?"

"Relax and finish your breakfast. I'll wake your brother." Mom smoothes my ponytail then puts her coffee on the table before leaving to attempt to wake David.

David is not coming with us I know. He'll stay home and play video games instead. I would bet twenty bucks on it but keep that thought to myself.

Breakfast is really good and I concentrate on every bite as I finish. Pushing visions of the hurricane and my dream away, I imagine what the lake will be like today.

Will there be a lot of people on boats or more swimming? Should I wear my bathingsuit from last year or the new one? I don't even know if the one from last year will fit because I grew two inches since last summer.

I am 5'7 now. Dad says if I grow another two inches, Uncle Leo will drag me to Hollywood to be the next top model but I would rather be an actress. Maybe start out in one of my uncle's series commercials then move on to bigger and better things like TV or movies.

Imagining what my first commercial will be, sudsy organic shampoo or an innovative new tech toy, I put my plate and fork in the dishwasher, wipe my hands on my napkin and walk out the front door to look for the girl and her dog.

They might live on our street. She *was* barefoot. I walk up

Wilson Ave, looking down driveways and into people's front yards. A lady gardening on her hands and knees waves at me with yellow gloves. I wave back nearly tripping over two little kids drawing on a driveway with sidewalk chalk. They giggle at me almost falling. Kids always laugh at that kinda stuff.

"Sorry!" I tell them noticing that one of the girls has the same kind of hair the girl with the dog has.

Ding. Ding. Ding. Clue number one.

"Hey, do you guys know where the curly haired girl around my age with the grey dog lives?"

"That's my sister and my dog," the curly haired girl looks up at me squinting in the sun. "But I can't tell you where we live because you're a stranger," she says extending her arm as far as it will go pointing her finger at me.

I look at her with sidewalk chalk on her nose and in her hair wondering if she is serious. She is.

"Uhmm, can you give her a message for me then?"

"Maybe. What is it?"

"Tell her to come back to where she found her dog, please."

The little girls look at each other and giggle again. They are about five or six years old.

"Oh kay!"

They giggle louder and go back to drawing hearts, dogs and cats on the driveway in blue, purple, yellow, and pink chalk.

"Thanks!" I say, "There's like no one my age in this neighborhood and I would like to meet her." I shuffle my bare feet back and forth on the hot sidewalk, smiling my best kid friendly smile.

They do not look back up.

Daffodil House is almost a block away from where they are drawing and I scan for the girl and her dog methodically looking in between every house and in all the driveways on the way back, walking on grass when I can to cool my hot feet.

Mom is waiting for me on the front step with her coffee, a quizzical look on her face. She is wearing running shorts, a tank top, and Haikus running shoes. Her shapely legs are pressed together at the knees.

Mom has great legs because she runs but she needs to do some pushups or something to get at that tricep arm flab. She's got it like way too early. Like a centaur, all her strength is on the bottom. But she is a Sagittarius moon though so that makes sense. Maybe I'll mention it.

"Where'd ya go?" Mom asks.

"I went looking for that girl and her dog," I say sitting next to her on the step. "She's probably the only girl in the neighbor- hood even close to my age."

Mom puts her arm around my waist. "Good idea. I'm sure you'll find her. This neighborhood is small enough to hear a pin drop."

Whatever that means.

Mom looks happy and well rested today.

Like the hurricane never happened. Like there was no oil spill.

"David is not coming with us, is he?"

"No, it'll be just us girls today," Mom says getting up and pulling me up with her. "Ready to go?"

I nod.

"Wanna get your bathing suit on, grab a towel and meet me in the kitchen in ten minutes. Can you be ready that fast?"

"I sure as shit can," I smile full teeth and wide eyed, trying to forcibly joke around with Mom even though I feel stressed.

"Lena!" my mother hisses looking around like she hopes no one else heard.

"Mom!"

"You are too pretty to curse so *please don't.*" "I'm just trying to be funny..."

"Please be funny without cursing. People might get the wrong idea..."

"Fine. Can we stop at Dandy Doughnuts on the way and get an iced mocha with whipped cream and chocolate chips?" I ask bouncing on my toes.

Mom nods and I run upstairs to get ready.

TEN

At the lake, every man around looks me up and down drinking me in like they're low on electrolytes and I'm a Gatorade. I am wearing a black bikini that barely covers my butt even though it's sports style.

Some of the ogling old dudes could be my Dad's friends. Eeesh. I round my back and pull my tee shirt down.

Shuddering, I hide behind Mom as she pays for the pedal boat and a guy dad's age cranes his neck to get a better look at my legs. Yuck. I should have worn a tunic. Making sure none of the old dudes see my ass when I bend over, I back into the boat and sit down.

The boat is a white swan with bench seats and bike pedals in the bottom. One skinny adjustable steering wheel is positioned in front of the driver's seat. It has a canopy top over the swan head to protect us from the sun. I sit in the driver's seat and quack the horn at Mom while she takes her sweet time getting in.

As soon as she's got both feet in the boat, I start pedaling. Mom teeters and falls back on the seat swatting my shoulder.

The lake is huge but way lower than it was last year. The floating docks measure about three feet lower and like a third of it is dammed off.

Still, a lot of people are enjoying what's left of it. Some are sailing, some are motoring, and some like us, are pedaling. I have a spike in energy because I finished my iced mocha with whipped cream and chocolate chips. I steer smoothly and we pedal around the entire lake once.

Caffeine and sugar power!

After one complete circuit, we stop to rest on the side of the lake in the shade of a large oak tree. Mom hands me a hydro flask to drink some water.

"How long do you think before we can drink the water and swim at the beach again?" I ask after my sip of mountain tap water which is still drinkable thankfully.

"I don't know, hon. Hopefully, soon."

Mom looks out over the lake. She takes her round red sunglasses off and wipes the lenses with her shirt. She wipes mascara smudge from under her eyes with a tissue from her pocket and looks at me apologetically.

"I think that's what your father and uncle want to talk to you about. They have an idea to make money off the water crisis with a substitute of some kind, called Wüter."

"Making money off the water crisis sounds awful." I scowl, passing the flask back to her. "Leave it to Dad to want to do something like that."

"Hm," Mom says thoughtfully knitting her brows. "I should have worded it better. What your father actually said was… they have a golden opportunity to invest in a product …based on need created by …water scarcity. Does that make sense?"

"It's okay, Mom. I know what you mean," I say looking over the boat into the shallow water where tiny fish dart in and out of algae. "But what do they want *me* to do?"

"Well you're the family actress. They want you to be in a commercial or a live infomercial or something. Your father was rushing to leave when he told me so I'm not quite sure what the format will be but I know it involves you… acting. Isn't that nice?"

"I guess so," I say watching the fish swim around a decaying soda can.

"You've had five school plays picked up by local TV."

"So."

"You even got fan mail, remember?" Mom smiles patting my knee.

"Mmmhm."

"So maybe…this is your big break. Your father and uncle think you can make a lot of money doing the commercial for their …

uh investment. *Plus* you'll be entering the family business doing something you love. Doesn't that sound better than theatre camp?"

"Moth-er!" I yell pulling my attention away from nebulous water life below and leaning my forehead on the steering wheel. "You *know* I want to be an actress but ... this water crisis is scary and now it's close to home. I mean it's directly affecting us and y'all are not very concerned. That scares me more than anything!" I say popping my head back up with a jolt. "What about Wilmington? We can't drink the water or swim down there anymore! The ocean is black! Have you seen it? Do you even care?"

My mother says nothing. Her mouth is pressed in a tight line. She looks away from me out over the lake.

"There are dead birds and fish all over the beach, Mother! Water restrictions are a level five over night! And what about our house? Is anyone gonna check on our fucking house? You're acting like it's no big deal! Business as usual!" I yell loud enough that people in other boats look over at us.

I cover my face with my hands and the swan boat begins making circles because no one is steering.

Mom puts her sunglasses back on, redoes her bun, applies lip balm, and smoothes her eyebrows. She folds her hands in her lap, stands to straighten her shorts, sits and folds her hands again. She fidgets when she is uncomfortable. I guess I made my point.

"Lena, steer the boat please," she practically whispers.

"Mother!" I yell putting one finger on the steering wheel. "I want answers!"

"I'm sorry but I don't have answers this time. I'm just a woman, a mother, an author trying to finish this book and raise my family."

"Mom, please?!" my voice breaks high pitched, verging on hysterical.

Mom puts her hand on my back.

"Honey, calm down. Look. We have good homeowners insurance and your father knows the agent. It's Sunday ... she'll check on the house tomorrow. That's one thing." Mom exhales deeply. "I agree. The water situation is scary... but what can we do about it? Hurricanes, floods, wildfires, earthquakes...extreme weather is normal.

If Wilmington is in good shape by the end of summer we can go home. If not... we might have to stay here awhile. The high school here... Celo High is smaller than what you're used to but you'd make friends fast. Remember, when we moved you to a new fourth grade? How quickly you adapted?"

"What?" I hiss. "I was eight! Little kids always make friends fast! It's not the same now. I'm going into eleventh grade. Eleventh grade! We have *groups* of friends now and we are not moving! Why are you even saying that? Are you trying to upset me more?"

I put both hands on the wheel and start to steer, veering sharply away from a beautiful sailboat named *Whales Tale* a boat length in front of us. The frantic couple in matching madras shorts on the *Whales Tale* stop waving their hands and shouting from the stern and the little boy sucking his thumb at the bow pulls it out of his mouth and gives me a thumbs up.

"Thank you," Mom says quietly.

"I am not moving, okay? And that's way beside the point. Dad said it's gonna cost billions of dollars to clean up down there. Who's gonna pay for that? This shit is insane."

Mom's face has turned a light grey blue like a heron. She scoops a handful of lake water and wets her neck with it. Her other hand rubs circles in the middle of my back, not even close to calming or reassuring.

"Why are you cursing so much today?" she asks softer than a southern belle looking at me like she has no idea who I am or where I came from.

"Who cares if I'm cursing?! I am talking about running out of clean water, Mother! That is way more important than a few words you don't like!" I swat her hand away.

"Fine," Mom says folding her hands in her lap. "Since you won't have it any other way, I'll level with you."

Bowing her head, she considers the position of her folded hands and readjusts them as if that will help with what she has to say. Inhaling and exhaling audibly, she clears her throat once too before leveling.

"The environmentalists in Wilmington, the protestors, are… are after your father and his partner even *more* now because of this new spill. A brick was thrown through the office window last night and he's been getting threatening phone calls and emails. Your father is the face of that company to many people even though he's only the lawyer. So even with cleanup under way, we might not be able to go back awhile …for safety reasons."

A fish jumps a few feet from our boat. Kids laugh. A mother scolds. People talk. A guy yells to his friends and they yell back. A boat motor starts. Someone jumps in the lake splashing. My ears are full of noise and movement.

I am crashing from the sugar and caffeine and reeling from this new information. Starting to feel spinny and separate from the world, I put my head on my knees and squeeze my eyes shut.

"Honey, let's go home. Your father and uncle will be there soon."

"Can you please steer?"

"Gladly."

We switch places. I keep my eyes closed and we pedal back to the dock in silence. My mind is working over time. Our beautiful beach ruined by oil. No swimming in the ocean, level five water restrictions, major contamination caused by Dad's top client.

Dad is getting threatening phone calls. What's the world gonna be like twenty years from now? Ten years from now?

A shiver runs down my spine so fiercely the boat rocks. Mom puts her hand on my hand. I hold back tears threatening a flood behind my walled eyes. I hold them back because if I let them go, I won't be able to stop.

ELEVEN

Mom heads straight to her office to work on her book as soon as we get back to Daffodil House, even though it's "Family Day."

She writes romance novels. Her last book, *Houston Heat* was a best seller two summers ago. The cover was hilarious; a hulking bare-chested guy with a tribal tattoo and a little woman with a tiny waist, red lipstick, and black shining hair. They were all pressed together life or death like with waist high water swirling around them in a flood.

I tried reading it but couldn't. As soon as I got to the first sex scene I felt so embarrassed that my mother wrote it, I had to stop.

Hanging in the office doorway, I watch my mother settle into writer's mode with a grateful sigh and the scary realization that neither of my parents is going to secure my future on a changing planet snarls at me energetically like a dark entity in the corner.

Feeling resentful of my parent's chosen professions and more than a little scared, my hardened eyes wander over Mom's office, which was Pop's office a long time ago. She never changed anything about it, just kind of plopped her laptop in there and moved in.

The walls are still decorated with framed family photos, naval awards, and a captain's hat. There are photos of Pop and Gram's wedding, Pop and Gram waving from a cruise ship, Mom eating cake on her first birthday, Mom's first day of school, Mom hugging a dog, Gram winning first prize at a county fair for 'best rose bush,' and Mom and Gram dressed in fancy dresses.

Mom insists that family memories are comforting and knowing her father sat here years before helps her writing. But I mean, come on? How in the world does sitting in your dead father's office help you write romance novels? Every living member of my family is hella fucking weird.

Playing judge hard right now, I catch myself detaching spiritually and say, "I am on Earth in a human body," which has kinda been my mantra since I was like five.

"What are you saying over there?" Mom asks positioning her black and white polka dot reading glasses and adjusting the computer screen. "Why don't you go see what your brother is doing? And close the door on the way out."

"Screw you, Mom. Thanks for caring!" is what I feel like saying but don't. Mom is being a serious escapist douchebag right now trading me, her real life daughter in, for characters in a book on the only day we ever get to do anything together! She snaps her headset into place, probably listening to opera, and starts typing before I can say anything else

Ok, Mom just brushed me off like a flea.

"Go see what your brother is doing," is a joke, of course. I know what he's doing.

He is either:

A. asleep

B. playing video games

When David is not surfing, sleep and virtual reality are his only priorities. We could be in the middle of the most interesting conversation or fun real-life event and David will sneak off to get game time in. He competes at high levels with people all over the world.

I flip Mom the bird with both hands and wave them around because I know she won't see me. She is in romance land with whatever characters she's made up this time. And because she wants me to leave right away, I don't. Instead, I place my right foot against my left thigh and stand in my favorite yoga pose, tree pose, observing her while she works.

Her light brown grey streaked hair curls around the red headset I bought her for Mother's Day. She says they are the most useful gift she has ever received. I am glad she likes them so much but sometimes when she uses them to tune me out, I feel like taking them right off her head and snapping them in two.

Of course that would not be nice and I never do it. But it is fun to think about what she would do if I did, what her expression might be like and stuff. I snicker softly holding a momentary vision of Mom's face aghast as I hand her back her broken headset in two dangling pieces.

Mom claps her hands to snap me back to attention. "Lena! You are zoning out! Go away please, I can't focus with you staring at me like that!"

She motions vigorously for me to close the door but does not look away from the screen. I would call that avoidance.

Still in tree pose, I do the other side real quick to make sure I am even then close the door nearly all the way but not all-all the way.

Walking down the narrow hall to my brother's room just for the hell of it; I marvel that the redwood floor Pop laid way before I was born never makes a sound, not one creak. This makes it easy to sneak up on people even when you are not trying to. When David and I were little, we played hide, seek and sneak attack and that's how I know.

I stop in front of David's door and knock, nose level with the hand printed sign that says, *"Do not enter gamer at play."* David does not answer.

I lean against the door and yell, "David? What are you doing?" As if I didn't know.

"I'm in the middle of warfare, woman! Go away," comes my brother's muffled voice over the sound of machine guns and computerized voices yelling, "Man down! Man down!"

I jiggle the doorknob. It is locked.

David has been "in the middle of warfare" for over two years now, since Mom bought him that stupid video game. There is always the next level or some new weapon that keeps him interested.

David wears a headset too with goggles attached. His is black. Sometimes he forgets to lock the door and I walk by and push it open with my foot and that is what I see every time; the back of his head with his black headset on in front of a huge screen playing that dumb war game. He sits in a swivel chair with his feet propped up on the console moving only his upper body. Once in a while he gets up and paces.

I bet video games have the power to hypnotize people who

play them all the time like this magician I once saw on a cruise ship.

He hypnotized a guy in the audience to think he was captain of the Titanic. The magician rang a bell and the guys face went blank, like David's when he plays the war game. Then the entranced guy ran around the room shouting orders and looking for his first mate. When the hypnotist clapped his hands, the guy snapped out of it and went back to his seat like nothing happened.

I clap my hands and whisper loudly, "David you are now awake!" Then I slump against the wall. Sadness and anxiety are creeping in around the corners of my mind. I am the only one in this family that cares about anything real. David and Mom would probably be fine drinking a water substitute.

Worldly weight setting on my shoulders, I slouch walk back down the hall and ooze down the spiral staircase to the cool, quiet kitchen. I open the refrigerator door. Milk, eggs, cheese, ham, turkey, celery, yogurt, mint, cucumber, sprouts, berries, bean salad, lettuce, and sprouted whole wheat bread in a bag. I close the refrigerator door.

I pour water from the tap into a glass and drink it. The meter behind the sink counts eight ounces.

I walk into the living room and pick up the TV remote control, sit on the couch and stare at the screen. I flip through channels. Commercial. Commercial. Commercial. Repeat of a Disney show. Repeat of Teen Mom. Commercial. Commercial. There is nothing on.

I turn around on the couch facing the window and pull aside the lacy cream-colored curtain. Sunlight warms my face. There are birds and squirrels in the yard. I watch a cat watching the birds peck the grass.

I miss my Grandmother, I miss my friends, and I am worrying.

Ughhh!!!

I throw my head back and scowl as hard as I can at the ceil- ing. The white ceiling fan spins around and around, silver pull chain dangling helplessly in the center.

Come on TV! I need a distraction!

I pick a random channel and it's a cooking show. The chef is measuring milk and melted butter for a quiche. The chef is a woman with red hair and a very big, bright red lipstick smile. The camera pans over a clapping audience and back to the red-haired smiling chef.

Mom and I took cooking lessons once. We learned how to make super thin crust New York style pizza from scratch and for a few months, I made pizza every Wednesday night. For incentive, Mom bought me a set of fancy kitchen tools and an apron that had the words, *Master Chef Lena* sewn on it in red. Red is

Mom's favorite color. Dark purple is mine but still Mom buys red for me like she doesn't know.

For a minute, I imagine myself as the smiling chef on TV wearing a purple apron. Then I change the channel.

An historic 8.9 measure Earthquake in Iran kills hundreds of people today. The flood in Texas continues and wildfires rage in Southern California. More on these stories next..."

I turn the TV off, heart thumping out of my chest. Maybe I should go outside.

"I wish you were here, Gram," I say. "I mean I wish you were here in a normal non-zombie, back from the dead kinda way."

One tear escapes my eye and slides down my cheek. It hovers on the edge of my upper lip and I lick it off. The salty taste reminds me of the ocean.

TWELVE

My legs take me through the kitchen to the back door where I turn the old crystal knob and step outside. There is no pool or trampoline, not even a swing.

Only an old birdbath, flower pots sitting upside down, two bags of old looking dirt, lots of freshly mowed thick green grass, roses of course, and a long trailing vine with white flowers on it which I can't remember the name of.

I am bare foot and the grass feels cool and inviting. I walk to the center of the yard. A dozen purple butterflies flutter up out of the green grass. I watch them fly over the fence and out of sight.

Sighing, I drop to my knees, to my hands then lie all the way down on Earth. My face, now close to Earth, is close enough to see little ants and pill bugs or "rolly-pollies" as Gram called them, working or playing or doing whatever it is they are doing.

The grass and Earth smell good, really good and I relax into it with a long exhale. I turn over to lie on my back and look up at the sky. Long thin, white, clouds slide and slink like a lazy parade. It is warm out but not hot, maybe 84 degrees, definitely not 90.

I look up at the sky for a long time until I see an airplane. An ant crawls on my arm and I flick it off. I turn back onto my stomach and prop up on my forearms holding my face in my hands. It feels good being this close to Earth.

"I welcome the power of *Earth* into my life," I say in a deep, calm voice I barely recognize. "I love *Earth.*"

As I speak I feel Earth energy spiraling in through my belly button, fusing with my own energy, and coming out my mouth, sweeter and deeper than my voice alone.

Maybe I'm imaging it but ... I am fifteen so my voice could be changing. I press my toes, belly, hands and face to Earth enjoying the calm, cool connected energy I feel.

Suddenly, the dream comes rushing back to me. The geese, the message. What did it mean?

"Ritual is the key to your birth gifts. You must welcome the elements as Earth's messengers and friends."

Welcome the elements? Like I just did? Like Earth, Air, Fire, Water, and Space?

Yes, yes, yes my intuition screams. *Create a ritual for each.*

"Sweetie, stop second guessing yourself. Be in universal flow and allow spirit to work through you and you will be fine. That was a

beautiful welcome to Earth element," Gram's voice comes crystal clear in my mind.

I push up, sit up virasana style, on my knees, and look around half expecting to see a hidden camera. Stranger things have happened. Just to be sure there isn't one, I get up and walk around the yard peering behind bushes and under the larger flowerpots.

No hidden camera.

I shake my head and rub my eyes. I pinch my arm.

"I'll add only this," Gram's flute like voice floats again into my mind. *"Without Earth, the human species would not exist. We must listen to and protect Earth. We welcome the power of Earth element as messenger of Planet Earth."*

I wonder if Gram is like tapping into my subconscious from the great beyond or heaven or wherever you go after you die, her voice is so clear.

"Without Earth, humans would not exist. We must listen to and protect Earth. I welcome the power of Earth element as messenger of Planet Earth," I recite.

"Good," says Gram's voice in my mind.

Confused but happy to be connecting with Gram, I picture her clearly. In the vision she is filling colorful, home-made bird feeders with seed. Birds, red, brown, blue, and black, flock around her waiting to eat.

Just as I vision her, the wind picks up. There was no wind before.

Zero wind.

The wind picks up from out of nowhere and the flowers and rose bushes sort of sway. Gram once said that after she died she would be a cool breeze on a warm summers day. She is making herself known to me.

Out of the corner of my eye I see a shimmer; a very faint iridescent shimmer, like a ripple in water but in the air. I also smell her warm cinnamon rose scent but only for a second. When I sniff the air again it is gone.

I am silent, still, alert. The little hairs on my arms and legs

stand up.

"Gram, if you are here can I see you please? I would like to see you."

I look for a long time scanning every inch of the yard. I don't see anything like Gram trying to step into this dimension or anything and nothing else interesting happens.

Aloud I say, "Today I welcome the five great elements, Earth, Water, Air, Fire, and Space, I welcome them as Earth's messengers and as friends."

This is not the normal me talking.

It is like I am being guided or used as a tool. Like something or someone is speaking through me. For a minute I consider running upstairs to tell Mom. But Mom would think I'm crazy or looking for attention.

Either way, she would take me back to Dr. Lanson, the pear-shaped grief counselor, who would ask 1000 questions, not listen to my answers, and suggest I take medicine. Medicine that would make me sick to my stomach and numb. I quickly dismiss the idea of telling Mom.

I mean, if it was any other dead person talking to me like this I would be totally freaking out but it is Gram and I love her. So this isn't scary just interesting and also I kinda wished for it. I am going to Gogle whether other people have had deceased relatives get into their minds and teach them things.

The 'all knowing Gogle'...funny I trust answers I find online. I wonder what percent of facts you find online are actually true?

Logic is a tactic I use when I am trying not to freak out. Kind of like a time out I give myself when I don't know what to do.

It sometimes works.

Ok, Gram. You are my favorite person in the world and I trust you in all forms. I do not fully understand what is happening and why right now but I am open to the experience," I say trying to use my deep, calm voice but it comes out in a sort of squeak instead.

Again the wind picks up where there was no wind before and the flowers and rose bushes sort of dance a little. Again I see a faint shimmer like the ripple of water but in the air. A shimmery sort of sparkly dust the sunlight plays off wavers near me but I can't make out a definite shape.

Clear as a bell in my head, Gram says, *"This is an important summer for you, Lena. The summer of fifteen has always been the summer women in our lineage are presented with full use of their gifts... if they have them. And you my dear have them. When your mother was born without telepathy or psychic ability, I worried that our lineage was weak or dying. When you were born, I knew why they skipped your mother...so that your gifts, granddaughter, would be potent, as potent as my own grandmother's, at a time when the world needs them."*

Another warm breeze sets the flowers and rose bushes to swaying again.

"Do you believe in reincarnation granddaughter?"

"I never really thought about it, Gram."

"Reincarnation of souls in ancestry is the way things work dear. It is how one accumulates karma...and I feel very strongly... that you and your great-great-grandmother's spirit are one and the same."

The light touch of a purple butterfly landing on my leg causes goose bumps to raise all over me. I stroke its wing gently once with the tip of my finger and it flies away.

"I do resemble her... I've seen pictures."

"She was a wonderful woman... communicating with intergalactic beings and traveling inter-dimensionally during a very important time in history. Women's Suffrage... and as this is also an important time in history, I believe you Lena Lenora, have come back with gifts even stronger than before."

"I don't feel gifted right now. I feel stressed and alone. None of my friends are like me... and I don't understand anyone in my living family like at all."

"You are an old soul in a teenage body, dear. You will not be

drawn to pop culture like less evolved souls. And even though you feel alone, you are not. There are many sensitive, gifted young people like you, they are just spread out and some try to hide or dull their gifts to fit in. But don't worry...soon you will have a friend, a gifted girl like you. She will be the first of many..."

"Wait. You are going to send me a friend?" I interrupt out loud.

"You will soon have a friend, yes. But I am not sending her to you. Your friendship was written in the stars long ago! You are Star Seeds on the same mission."

"Mission? Gram, please. You mean an actual living girl like me right, not a spirit like you?"

"Yes, dear, an actual living girl like you with similar ancestry. May I continue?"

"Yes, sorry. I just ...I need a friend here. I might really go crazy if I have to spend another day alone with Mom and David who's only 'mis- sion' is to escape reality whenever they can. I don't think anyone in my living family but me cares about anything real."

"It is an equally scary and fascinating time to be alive on Earth and escape is the choice of many so don't be hard on them. It's all part of the plan, which soon you will come to know. All of the best things in life happen at just the right time, don't you agree?"

"But you died, Gram and it wasn't the right time for me. I wanted you around forever, at least until I graduated college."

"The human body doesn't last forever, Lena, not even healthy ones.

But I will always be with you in spirit whenever you need me."

Another warm breeze, this one with a touch of cool in it, causes the porch wind chimes to gong, tinkle, and ting a melody

like fairies dancing in rain. A squirrel climbs the bird feeder to find no seed. A white cat with a grey patch on its chest jumps on the fence watching the squirrel. Puffy white clouds roll across a bright blue sky. Bees dive deep into roses open fully to the sun and I am having an important conversation with my dead grandmother.

"I miss the living you so much, Gram. You were the only one in the family I ever really identified with. I mean, I'm glad you're here even if you are just a voice in my head right now which is… a little weird. I mean if it was anyone else I would definitely be scared."

"Oh, honey, let's jump to getting past that now, okay? We've always been able to communicate telepathically even when you were little, remember?"

"It's my first memory," I tell her telepathically, smiling.

"You were three, in the garden like you are now. You told me you loved the smell of roses best and I said I did too. Such a simple first mind exchange and so very special."

"Yea," I remember dreamily feeling very small. A part of me wishes I could go back to that time when there was no stress or worrying. Let the adults take care of everything! But the adults are *why* there is pollution and water scarcity everywhere so now the weight is on me and my generation to do something about it.

"Stay positive, granddaughter. Blame is a low vibration and it

will lower yours," Gram corrects. *"Keep focusing on the present in a positive light and ask how you can help. That is the only way. Now, if you sit quietly for a few minutes every day when you wake up and every night before you go to sleep, you will feel much better during this time of intense change and heightened awareness. It will help you digest all the things so they don't clutter your mind. Being grounded yet open mentally and spiritually is what you're aiming for. You might not know it yet but you are an important person and we need you at your best in every way."*

"I should write into Kiki Astromatrix and tell her she was right about big changes."

"Who?"

"Kiki Astromatrix. She's my favorite astrologer. She forecasted big changes for Aquarius rising, big changes for Taurus too, and she was right. She's always right."

"You might not want to broadcast personal things especially of this nature. But it's up to you as with everything. Now, promise me you'll take daily quiet time to digest all the new?"

"Meditation is the least of my worries right now, Gram, but yes I promise, I will. Hey, what's it like over there, in the spirit world?" I ask genuinely interested but feeling sort of silly like the time I requested a picture from the tooth fairy and nothing happened.

"It is quite lovely. But it takes a lot of energy to be back in the third dimension with you, dear. I only have enough to guide you and help you along in the mission."

"I'm fifteen, Gram. I don't even understand half of what you're saying. I mean, I get some of it but what am I supposed to...?"

"All will be revealed in time. Just concentrate on your ritual welcoming of the elements today, please. Oh, and do me a small favor? Fill the bird feeders and clean out the birdbath. I want birds to feel welcome here."

"Okay," I say out loud, suddenly tired. I rub my face and head with my hands. My head is so full, but I feel loved in the presence of Gram and I haven't felt that way since she died so I know it's really her. I know I am not crazy.

"When will I meet my new friend," I ask wanting to continue the conversation. Gram doesn't answer. She must be gone.

I am about to go inside and research whether other people have had deceased relatives get into their minds and teach them things when a large red bird lands in the birdbath.

There is no water in it, only leaves and an old decomposing newspaper. The red bird looks directly at me and squawks loudly. It hops, tips its head in annoyance, ruffles its feathers, and flies away swooping low over my head.

I roll back and forth a couple of times then somersault backwards up into standing. I pull over the green plastic trashcan, the one used for sticks and leaves and stuff. I scoop out the leaves and newspaper from the birdbath and dump them into the trashcan. It comes out in one big wad.

I go into the kitchen, fill a mason jar with water, and watch the meter's little red ball go up and up. 16 ounces. Transporting fresh water from the kitchen tap to the birdbath this way three times, I use 48 ounces total, dumping the water into the bird- bath. I step back to look at my work, hoping the red bird will return.

One gray cloud appears in the sky. Then another. Raindrops join the tap water in the birdbath. It is raining and sunny: a sun shower!

I place my pointer finger in the birdbath and walk around and around making circles in the water. The raindrops create their own movement. It is mesmerizing.

I stare at the ripples the raindrops make allowing myself to relax completely, starting to digest everything that's happened in the past 24 hours.

"I welcome the power of *Water* into my life, I love Water. Without clean water there is no life. Water must be protected. I welcome the power of Water element as Earth's messenger and friend," I hear myself say. My voice is calm and confident.

The rain, falling hard and fast now, plasters my hair to my fore-head and drips from my nose while I stand by the birdbath with my finger in the water thinking about having a friend. The rain is warm and makes everything smell clean and fresh.

Lifting my face to the sky, I walk around the yard tasting the warm rain and sun. My feet squish in the grass. Little puddles form around them. The rain slows and then stops.

The sun shines strong and bright and the grey clouds roll away. The white cat with a gray spot on his chest reappears on the fence. He looks at me. I look at him. The cat licks its paw. I wring out my hair, wipe my feet on the mat, and go inside.

THIRTEEN

In the house, nothing has changed but me. Mom is still cocooned in her office working on her book and David is stowed away in his room in VR world.

But everything *feels* different because *I* am different. An electric buzz running from the base of my spine all the way to the top of my head, connects every nerve ending on the way. Alight on the inside, the agitated anxiety I felt earlier has transformed into a sort of stoic determination.

The quiet house no longer irritating, welcomes me with the pleasant hum of silence like a clear path towards the days quest. I retreat to my lilac room... thoughtfully, dripping rainwater.

My room was Mom's room when she was little. When I was born it became mine in summer and whenever I visited. On my third birthday, Gram asked me to pick a color for the walls. I picked lilac and that's the color the walls are still. I had good taste at three.

The lilac room is pretty when it's neat and clean. There is an antique vanity with a mirror and drawers, a matching bureau, a small desk, a window seat with a cushion, and of course, a bed.

I haven't unpacked a thing yet so new things and old things are all mixed up making a very disorganized, unwelcoming mess. Clothing and boxes, magazines, books, and art supplies from last year, even the year before, are scattered everywhere.

You could call it chaos.

I need to clean it ... now.

After I change, I pick up my things one by one and unpack my suitcase. I place the dirty clothes in the laundry chute, fold the clean clothes and put them away according to color in the closet and according to whether they are tops or bottoms in the dresser drawers.

My underwear and socks go in the small drawers in the middle, tops go in the large top drawer and bottoms in the large bottom drawer. Then I put all of the things I no longer want in a box for Goodwill. I completely clear the floor and vacuum the rug. I clear and organize my desk and window seat. I wipe down all the furniture, change the sheets on my bed and wash the quilt.

It takes me two hours. Now my room is clean and clutter free. I feel inspired.

Unrolling my turquoise yoga mat, I place it in the middle of the ancient green and gold rug that Gram and Pop brought back from India before Mom was even born. I do a perfect somersault, rise like a gymnast arms wide to an invisible audience.

I forward fold, jump back into plank, move into upward facing then downward facing dog again for one complete sun salutation and lower onto my belly. I stretch out long in all directions, enjoying the open space in my newly cleaned room. Pressing myself up on to hands and knees and then into a downward facing dog again, I walk my feet to meet my hands at the top of the yoga mat. Then I reverse swan dive towards the sky ending in mountain pose.

Aloud I say, "I welcome the power of *Space* element into my life. I love Space."

Space has another name too, like the elemental word for space… something funny. What is the other word for space? I try hard to remember.

"Oh ya! Ee- thur! Ether!" I burst out, pleased. "All elements come from Ether. It is the origin of everything. It offers the space to form new ideas. Ether, open space must be protected! We 'hold space' for people so they can gather their thoughts. I welcome Ether as Earth's messenger and as friend."

My newly clean window seat is about four feet away. I wonder if I can make it there in one jump. I try and miss by a little more than a foot, making a louder than anticipated bang on the floor. Then I lunge onto the window seat as slowly and quietly as possible. I sit down cross-legged and look outside.

I can see the birdbath from here. Happy birds are bathing and drinking from it. I watch them, one red and one brown, dip their beaks, flutter their wings and splash in the water.

I open the window and fresh air wafts in. The air conditioning vent is just out of reach so I pull my desk chair over and stand on my tiptoes to close it. Wasting electricity is not conscientious.

"I welcome the power of *Air* into my life. I love Air," I say tapping my chest and inhaling deeply.

Fresh air always makes me feel more awake and alert. Prob- ably there is more oxygen in it than recycled air-conditioned air. How would Air element like to be welcomed?

I sit in the window seat letting my thoughts settle until the right words come.

"Ahhhaaa!" Air whooshes out of me with inspiration, "Air is the life force, the movement behind all, the start of all begin-nings. Without clean air, we would get sick and die. I welcome Air element into my life as Earth's messenger and as friend. We must listen to and protect Air. I love Air."

Not as poetic as I'd like, but it's true and will do.

I look out the window at the summer sky. It is changing the way it does before the sun and the moon trade places: pink to peach, blue to purple, and purple to gold.

My cell phone chimes.

A text from Sierra, *"Hi girl! We're safe! In PA at g-parents. Going to DE beach house next week. Might stay the summer bc of water. Not sure yet. How you? Ok?"*

Omygosh! Finally!

I text back, *"In Celo and ok. Miss you guys! Send pics!"*

"Send pics of your brother!" Sierra texts back with an animated cartoon of her head rolling and laughing.

Sierra used to have a crush on David when she was little. She doesn't now but sometimes jokes about it. I send her an animated version of my own head laughing then put the phone down.

I need to welcome one more element today to complete the ritual.

Fire. Fire is the final element and who can forget about fire?

But how am I gonna do that?

An image of a lit candle clearly appears in my mind. Okay.

I close the window, open the AC vent again and head downstairs to look for one of gram's homemade beeswax candles.

Mom is in the kitchen putting away dishes and talking on her cell phone.

"Mo-om," I sing song, "Where are the beeswax candles Gram used to make?"

"Why, hon?" Mom asks putting a finger up in the hold on gesture before saying, "We'll see you tomorrow then. Thanks for the call," into the phone. "Uncle Leo's flight was canceled due to heavy smoke. He'll take a private plane from another airport in the next few hours. Should be here in the morning."

"Smoke?"

Mom puts the phone on the table, takes out the clean silver- ware caddy, and begins putting spoons, knives, and forks away. "Apparently the smoke is so thick from the wildfires over there, the pilots can't see. They're rerouting people to surrounding airports until visibility is better."

"The wildfires are that bad?"

"Sadly, yes. Every year it gets worse. There's so much extreme weather right now it's hard to keep track. Did you hear about the earthquake in Iran?"

"Yeah," I say quietly leaning into the counter watching Mom put spoons away then wipe her hands on a kitchen towel.

"Is it safe to even go over there then... I mean with all the fires and smoke?"

"I doubt the fires will ever reach L.A. but we'll keep an eye on it, okay?"

"Okay."

"Speaking of fires, did you ask me about a candle?"

"Yeah. I wanna use one of Gram's beeswax candles tonight."
"What's wrong with your little desk lamp?"

"Desk lamps don't purify the air, Mom. The beeswax candles

Gram made smell good *and* purify the air. My room could use it, it smells like it's been closed up all year."

"It *has* been closed up all year."

Mom looks at me blinking like a mole coming out of earth for the first time in months. "I know you're responsible, but candles can be dangerous. A family I know burned their home down from a lit candle and my college roommate lit her canopy on fire with a candle...while she was in it!"

I can tell she is considering saying 'no' because of the way she is tilting her head and narrowing her eyes. When Mom is about to say 'no' that's the face she makes. Time for an interception.

"Your roommate lit her canopy on fire? Like her bed canopy?"

She nods.

"Wow, that sounds scary and I'm sorry it happened," I say in my most adult tone feeling older and wiser than poor Mom who was born without any psychic insight at all.

I put my hand on Mom's shoulder and look in her eyes, completely propelled by my mission to welcome *all* of the elements today.

"I promise I will blow the candle out before bed...and we can put the glass lantern over it too ... to keep it contained. Plus come check on me before you go to bed, if you want," I smile winningly knowing Mom won't check on me, she'll fall asleep reading like she always does.

"Deal," she says sticking out her hand, which I shake once firmly. "I believe your grandmother kept them in the dining room cupboard. "Should be holders in there too, if I remember right."

I run to the cupboard and fling open the bottom doors. The yummy clean scent of beeswax jumps out, ready for some air purifying action already. A taper candle wrapped in thin brown paper with a drawing of a bee on the front literally rolls forward towards my hand. Pick me! I want to welcome *Fire* the final element, it seems to say.

The glass lantern and brass candleholder are in there too. Plucking the three items, I close the doors, unwrap the candle and hold it to my nose. "Mmmmm," I breathe inhaling the delicious clean scent of beeswax.

"Purification, huh? You *are* your Grandmother's child," Mom says taking a whiff of the golden candle herself. "Do beeswax candles really do that?" she asks raising an eyebrow, "purify   the air?"

I nod, "Mmhmm and scented store-bought candles actually *pollute* the air like traffic 'caus paraffin comes from oil and then they add chemicals to make 'em smell good."

"If I knew that I forgot," Mom admits. "I'm all for clean air, it's more a matter of safety. But if you put it in the brass holder and keep the lantern over it, I feel better about it. Still remember to blow it out, ok I think those taper candles burn for around 12 hours."

"I'll blow it out! Don't worry!" If I wasn't holding the lantern and candleholder right now I'd be face palming my forehead.

Breathing in, I am relaxed. Breathing out, I am calm.

"Honey, don't get upset with me for being cautious.   That's what mothers are for." Mom raises my chin and looks me in the eye.

Jees! You'd think I was ten or something and not responsible at all the way Mom handles all of my decisions big to small.

When honestly, I feel like the most responsible person in the entire family!

But I don't want to fight right now so instead of shouting, "Whatevs, Mom! I am suuuuper responsible!" I shake it off and say in the most patient voice I can muster, "Okay, Mom. You're the Mom, Mom."

I smile baring my teeth and raising my eyebrows in quick succession like this ancient black and white TV star, Groucho Marx, hoping she will laugh.

She doesn't though, just presses her lips together and follows me up to my room. When the candle is in the brass holder on my window seat, she lights it then covers it with the glass lantern. Then she turns around and surveys my neat and clean room.

"Lena!" Mom exclaims forming a large O with her mouth, "I haven't seen your room look this good ...ever!" She plants a kiss on my forehead, "I hope you keep it like this all summer."

I smile at Mom. Mom smiles at me. She ruffles my hair then

smoothes it before walking out the door, "I'll check on you in a little while."

No, she won't. "Good Night, Mom."

Closing the door in front of her, Mom steps backwards into the hall. I breathe a sigh of relief.

Finally!

I close the AC vent again and turn off the desk light. I open the window.

The candle flame dances delightfully with the incoming waft of air. I inhale luxuriously. Ahhhh. Fresh air, candlelight and my clutter free room. This day is ending way better than it started.

My shadow self on the wall looms large and I gesture

grandly, sweeping my arms upwards in a wide arcing motion. My long hair splays out. I lift my face towards the ceiling and beyond that towards the sky, moon, and stars.

"I welcome the power of *Fire* and *Natural Light* into my life." I say in my deepest, calmest, most powerful voice yet. "I love Fire and natural light."

The soft orange and yellow candle flame glows and dances. It shape-shifts and flickers into a dancing lady, into a face with dark eyes, into a rearing horse, back into a flame.

I gaze into it.

"What is the welcome for Fire?" I know this one.

Taking a moment before welcoming Fire, the final element, I envision my beloved ancestor, Gram making the candle.

"*Fire* is the Great Digester. Call to Fire when something no longer serves. Fire helps metabolize food in the body and thoughts and impressions in the mind. Call to Fire for clarity, insight, and focus. Fire is powerful and must be respected. I welcome Fire element as Earth's messenger and as friend."

I sit down cross-legged, chin in hands staring into the candle flame. A light new tingly energy surrounds me like an invisible shield. Something unseen has shifted. Ancient memories stir but I can't remember what. The power of ritual and a mission complete clings to me like the strength and satisfaction of new muscle.

Tossing my pillow on the floor for quiet time like Gram suggested, I gaze into the candle flame for twenty minutes or so trying not to think.

But I do think.

I think of all the people who died in the earthquake. I think of the wildfires and of Uncle Leo and Dad coming tomorrow. I think of the hurricane we barely escaped. I think of Gram saying I am an important person and need to stay clear. I think of writing into Kiki Astromatrix and what I will say. I think of how nice it would be to take a bath right now and wonder if I'll ever take one again.

Then I let those thoughts fade away and just gaze into the flame and breathe.

When my eyes get heavy, I blow out the candle and jump into bed, falling asleep right away.

FOURTEEN

Monday 7:33AM. "Knock, Knock. Good News, hon!" Mom shouts from outside my bedroom door. I flash my eyes open with a start. I cannot stand waking up fast. It gives me a headache. I am irritated but Mom enters smiling like she won a contest or something.

"Wha-aattt?" I ask grumpily.

"I found out who the girl is and where she lives!" Mom says doing a little victory dance on the rug. "Her name is Sofia and she is your age. She and her family just moved here from Montana and I mean *just* this week!" Mom looks like a girl scout who just sold out of cookies, that happy.

"Really?" I rub my eyes and sit up. "You found out where she lives?"

"Two blocks over in the culdesac, the turquoise house with the huge wrap around porch and wild lawn. You can't miss it. It's the only house in the neighborhood with knee high grass," Mom bows beaming. Boy is she playing it up.

"Did you find out anything else?" I ask.

Mom's eyes sparkle as she continues doing the victory dance. She is wearing a black skort and a sweaty pink tank top. Her hair is pulled back in a ponytail. A headset hangs around her neck. She must have gone running.

"She has a little sister and a dog and ... they live with their father and aunt. The mother has an addiction problem and was causing issues for them in Montana so... they moved here ... for a fresh start."

Wow. Leave it to Mom to find out all of the details even the ones you don't want to know.

"What kind of addiction?"

"Ruthie Goldbarm, your grandmother's dearest friend's daughter, the one who knows everything that goes on within a mile, says the mom is or was addicted to...pills. Pharmaceuticals... painkillers or opiates or something."

Deflating a little passing the gossip, Mom's victory dance slows to a side to side, two step.

Gees. I stare at Mom not knowing what to make of the extra information and deciding to not do anything with it.

"Ok. Well, good work. Ill go over today and introduce myself."

"Good girl."

Mom hugs me and ruffles my hair. I hug her back patting her bony spine.

"Oh, and your father and Uncle Leo are here… in the kitchen having coffee."

"Uncle Leo's here? Now?"

"They've been here about an hour, pretty excited about this new business venture. This Wüter product. Why don't you get dressed and I'll make you a grapefruit juice. Meet you in the kitchen," Mom says backing out the door.

As soon as she leaves, I crawl to the center of the rug for a brief meditation before my shower. A promise is a promise.

AFTER MY SHOWER, I dress carefully knowing my Hollywood uncle is downstairs. Choosing a mid-length turquoise romper and a yellow cardigan to throw over my shoulders. I accentuate with a turquoise and gold necklace that was my grandmothers and complete the look with turquoise stud earrings. I carefully comb my long hair, part on the side, and let it hang loose down my back.

The only makeup I ever wear is brow gel and mascara because I have blond eyebrows and lashes you can hardly see. So I apply those and a peach lip balm that's also an SPF. Then I walk down the spiral staircase slowly, sensing that life is about to change... even more.

A few steps before crossing the kitchen threshold, I pause squeezing my eyes shut, to collect myself. I have wanted this opportunity for a long time, to be in one of my Uncle's commercials, on TV, in the movies and I knew this conversation would eventually happen but I don't feel ready.

What if I'm not ready?

Why does everything have to happen at once?

I have got to write in and tell Kiki Astromatrix all the stuff before I forget exact timing. Exhaling and inhaling slow and complete, I make a quiet lion's face, jump up and down a few times to pep myself up, and walk into the kitchen head held high, smiling like the president's wife.

"Lena! Well, well! I haven't seen you since you were knee high to a grasshopper!"

Uncle Leo, impeccably dressed in crisp chinos and a shimmering sapphire short sleeve shirt, stands to greet me as I enter the kitchen.

A gold chain nestling in his dark chest hair sparkles brightly like the sapphire (is that a sapphire?) pinky ring on his left hand. His slim tan belt matches the soft, shiny leather of his shoes perfectly. His teeth are astonishingly white.

"You really are turning into a beautiful young woman," he says scanning me methodically head to toe, pausing to look at my hair, eyes, mouth, hands, legs, and feet. "Great outfit," he says, "love the turquoise."

"Hi, Uncle Leo!" I say brightly, standing very tall and straight.

My uncle is as smooth as a seal and golden tan, handsome but with no warmth in his eyes when he smiles. A few inches shorter than my father but somehow much more intimidating.

Uncle Leo is my dad's older, half-brother. They have the same mother but different fathers. Leo's father was French Italian whereas my father's father was Scot Irish. My father has dark blonde hair and ice blue eyes and Uncle Leo has brown hair and coffee brown eyes.

They look nothing alike aside from the fact that they are both athletic, balding on top, and have a similar look in their eye when money is involved.

I give my uncle a quick hug. He smells like new leather, woodsy cologne and expensive moisturizer.

"I've enjoyed watching you as lead actress in your school plays," Uncle Leo says. "I'm sorry I couldn't get here to watch the last two in person. I've been extremely busy at the studio

and building a paradise in the Surin Islands in whatever free time I can scrape up."

"Thank you! Did you see them on YouTube or TV?"

"I saw them on YouTube but I know they were picked up by local TV too. Great work."

"Thanks."

"You're a natural actress, you know, very believable. Do you like acting?"

I nod a little too enthusiastically, "I do. It's fun."

"And you never get nervous with everyone watching you?"

"Not really. I mean sometimes I get butterflies but I like that." I shrug. "I just like practice my lines a lot ...and then they just come out."

"That's what all the great actresses say." He sits down and crosses a leg exposing peach socks with sapphire blue kites on them.

"I like your socks."

"Thank you, my assistant picked them out," Uncle Leo says looking down at his own socks and swinging his shiny shoe back and forth. "I will pass along the compliment to her, she really does a great job."

A smile and nod.

Uncle Leo smiles. "Lena, only niece. My own goddaughter! I'm so proud of the young woman you have become. You *are* a natural beauty with elegance and grace as well as a talented actress."

"Thank you," I say blushing.

"We've all known since you were little you would be an actress. We watched you glow on stage and light up the room with your little presence. But..." he pauses dramatically looking around, "you'll never get anywhere here in North Carolina. You'd have to move to Los Angeles to make a career of it."

"A career?" My eyes widen and I pull my head in and up like a meerkat sensing a hawk about to swoop. "I do want to be an actress but I'm fifteen, Uncle Leo, still in high school."

"What grade will you be in September?" "Eleventh."

"And you'll be 16 next April, correct?" "May."

"My agency works with teens and children of all ages." "Really? What kind of acting do they do?"

"All kinds! Why just last week we filmed a commercial for Durabell All Weather tires with two four-year-olds. Great kids, great moms, great people. They had a blast and the commercial turned out...perfect. Look for it in about a week on all major news and weather channels. It's being edited now."

My uncle smiles at me calculatingly. "I've been telling your parents for years, start her young, build a savings. It's as easy as that and believe me, darlin' I can spot a natural a mile away. As soon as I saw you dancing in the theatre at five, I knew."

"Really?"

"Really," he nods affirmatively. "But your parents wanted to wait. They didn't want you growing up in Hollywood. They wanted to give you a...a normal childhood." Uncle Leo raises an eyebrow. "Whatever normal means these days. But we've waited long enough and the time is right now. Fifteen is actually old to start an acting career. In Hollywood we say, ten today, forty tomorrow. Time flies. You grab your chance when it comes because it might not come again."

Dad clears his throat. "Leo is right. Time flies. If you're serious about pursuing acting, there's no time like the present. Especially with this guy as your uncle!" Dad claps Uncle Leo on the back.

Uncle Leo claps Dad on the back harder. Dad's wince evolves into a chuckle and he sits down at the kitchen table looking over at his brother, a mix of admiration and apprehension on

his face. It is clear Dad is second seed to his older brother and that alone amazes me.

"Have a seat, kiddo. Your Uncle and I have a proposition for you."

"Can you please not call me that, Dad?"

"So, what you're saying is you're too old to be called kiddo but too young to start an acting career," Dad laughs at his own joke and Uncle Leo laughs harder.

I sit down slowly feeling flattered, curious, and cautious.

Mom has placed a cheery yellow tablecloth on the wooden kitchen table and a clear vase full of white roses in the middle. A glass of grapefruit juice sits waiting for me and I reach for it.

Mom puts her hand on my shoulder for a second and refills the coffees in front of Dad and Uncle Leo before excusing herself to work on her book.

Uncle Leo sets his briefcase on the table, the same smooth tan leather as his shoes and belt. He smiles at Mom on her way out, "Thanks for the coffee, Doreen."

Then he opens his briefcase and pulls out what looks like a bottle of water.

"This," Uncle Leo says, "is Wüter, a water substitute scien- tists have been working on for over a decade. They finally got it right and just in the nick of time."

He pauses for effect patting the bottle like a puppy.

"Are you aware that at this very moment more than seventy percent of available freshwater left on this planet is too polluted to drink?"

Uncle Leo slides the Wüter in front of me smiling like a shark with a diamond in its mouth.

"I didn't know it was that much but I know it's bad and getting worse. And. it makes me super anxious," I say putting

my face in my hands. My head bumps the Wüter, which rolls back and forth on the table.

"Now, now," corrects my father, "being anxious only makes matters worse. When life gives you lemons, you make lemon-aid! Isn't that what Mom taught us, Leo?"

"I think with Mom, lemons meant money, Dave," Uncle Leo says chuckling. He taps the back of my head with one manicured finger and I look up. My uncle slides the Wüter in front of me again.

Holding back tears with a gulp, I steal a glance at my father who nods then looks back at Uncle Leo who folds his hands GodFather style and leans in.

"I understand your anxiety, Lena. Worrying about the water problem...is reasonable," says my uncle. "But your father and I are heavily invested in this product. I've been invested all along and your father well...he's all in now too. We stand to make a lot of money on this product, this Wüter. And when you have money, you don't need to worry as much about things like water pollution because, well money keeps you safe."

Uncle Leo's dark eyes glitter with greed. He studies my face. When I say nothing, he continues. "What I mean is, when you have alot of money, you will always be able to buy water or quench your thirst somehow. So you don't need to be... overly anxious. Does that make sense?"

I stare at my uncle and father who are looking at me like I'm a match that won't light and they need a fire.

"But why would anyone want to drink a water substitute?" I flick the bottle with my nail distastefully.

"Because water is polluted and getting worse. Water may be a thing of the past... already!"

"But what if we focus on cleaning up and protecting water rather than promoting a water substitute? Wouldn't that be better for everyone? Like... what about my kids and grandkids?"

"You're kids and grandkids? Are you planning on having them anytime soon?" Dad smiles the billboard smile totally down-playing my question.

A hot blush burns my cheeks.

Uncle Leo sits back slowly, shaking his head. He sips his steaming coffee, pinky up, peering at me with squinted eyes.

I turn to my father.

"Dad!" I insist. "What if we focus on cleaning up water instead? You and Uncle Leo could invest in ... water revitalization in Wilmington. We could make a commercial for that. You, you would both be like, like ... local heroes!?"

Dad and Uncle Leo make disgusted faces like a homeless person took a poo in the corner, wiped with their hand, then asked for money. My suggestion was that distasteful to them.

"Because sweetie," my father says collecting himself with a small cough, "to be honest, I would rather be rich than a hero. Our family has, for many generations, thrived on big business, and you will too. Besides if *we* don't invest in and promote this water substitute someone else will. The world needs a water substitute like it needs oil and chemicals. Consumerism will *never end*. I know you're young and it's scary but you'll thank me one day. I promise."

The possibility of running out of clean water makes me sad and afraid and also angry... but I don't say so again. I feel myself starting to float out of my body but I fight to stay in it. Picking up the Wüter, I open the cap, and smell it's sort of fake sweet, plastic-y scent.

"Have you guys tasted it?"

"We've tried it. It's not so bad. It sort of *grows* on you," says Uncle Leo winking, a slow smile spreading across his face. "Why don't *you* try it and tell us what *you* think."

My stomach is in a knot and doing somersaults. I wish I could run away from this conversation, run away from polluted water and the big business roots on this side of my family.

I wish Gram was alive so we could stand together on this or Mom was at least interested... but she's not, she'd rather write a romance novel. It's just me and that's the reality of it.

I inhale slowly and exhale even slower. Saying a silent prayer to never run out of clean water, I tip the bottle to my lips and drink the Wüter.

"It's not bad," I hear myself saying. "It's a little thicker than water and a tad sweet." I put the bottle back on the table and replace the cap. I didn't drink very much of it, maybe an ounce.

Without missing a beat, Uncle Leo says, "Your father and I would like to fly you to Los Angeles Friday. We're hosting a press conference on Wüter with the five o'clock news. We'd like you to be there. Tell the people you love it, that you prefer it over regular water. It'll be perfect because you're from Wrightsville Beach, where the chemical and oil spills are. It will touch people's hearts."

"But everybody in Wilmington knows my father is Chemican's lawyer." I say mortified.

"Don't sweat the small stuff, kiddo. Your father and I think you're perfect for the spot and like we said, we stand to make *alot* of money on this product. And if you're the spokesperson, *you'll* likely never have to worry about money ... ever." He laughs, crosses his legs the other way, and swings his tan leather shoe confident and comfortable, not a care in the world.

"We'll set up an account for you and let the money flow in. How does that sound?" Dad interjects. "You can buy a cool car when you turn sixteen, take your friends on vacation, whatever you want. With your talent and our pull, this could be the beginning of a great career for you."

"So don't you worry about a thing. Just smile, recite your lines and your father and I will take care of the details," Uncle Leo finishes with a flourish of his hands, no laugh lines or expression marks anywhere on his face.

Botox Face, I think...a crap ton of it. What else does he get done I wonder as his cell phone rings, Frank Sinatra's "Fly Me to The Moon."

"Excuse me I have to take this," Uncle Leo says bowing briefly at me. His pressed chinos swish crisply on the way out.

Dad covers my hand with his. "You don't look happy. What are you thinking?"

"Dad, I'm grateful for the opportunity and I love you," I mumble looking down at my hands, "but what about my future... like on the planet? Not just having money to buy stuff, but like having clean drinking water... when I'm your age?"

"Oh 'cumon hon, don't worry so much! They'll figure something out by the time you're my age, I am sure of it. Til then, might as well make a buck off it, huh? Water scarcity is a growing trend! Besides this is a great opportunity for you to get involved in the family business the way you want. Acting!"

Dad ruffles my hair downplaying my concerns again as if we live on two different planets and maybe we do.

"If you say no, you might not get another opportunity. That's not pressure, babe. Just logic. This commercial will open doors for you, the kind of doors you want opened." He lifts my chin, looks me in the eye, and touching the tip of my nose with his finger says, "Dink."

There's that money look.

I finish my grapefruit juice and stare at the Wüter. Tiny bubbles float to the surface. Shivering, I push my chair back and stand.

"I'm going for a bike ride," I announce. "There's a girl my age in the neighborhood and I wanna meet her. You guys go to breakfast without me, okay? I am not hungry."

"So, you'll do the commercial then?"

"Probably, ya," I screech halfway out the door. "I just ... I wish it was for something I was happy about. I mean I want to be able to swim in the ocean and drink real water, Dad."

"I understand completely! But we also have to be realistic." My father's ice blue eyes flickering with the money look get a little colder as I hold his gaze.

"This is so sad," I whisper too low for him to hear. Then I nod aggressively pulling up my best business voice. "Give me 24 hours to decide."

FIFTEEN

Rummaging in the garage for David's old bike, I cannot get away from the house fast enough.

If I begin my acting career with a commercial for a water substitute...won't that make me as bad as Dad and Uncle Leo? Won't that make me as bad as the chemical companies?

In my haste to escape compounded by anxious headspace, I trip over an orange tent and bang my head against an old golf cart hiding under a protective gray tarp.

"Owowowow!" I yell feeling the lump on my head begin to swell. I jump around a few minutes making faces until the pain subsides then I turn the key sitting in the ignition. It starts easily. "Oooh," I say momentarily distracted.

Maybe later I'll have a friend to ride it with. Rubbing my poor head, I imagine us zipping around the neighborhood in that thing. It's easy to drive.

Gram taught me to drive it last summer. The first hour I drove super slow for safety, which is good because I drove up on a lady's lawn and backed into a fire hydrant. But Gram never yelled she just laughed and laughed, holding onto her hat and warning people, "Watch out! My granddaughter is learning to drive!" A spider crawling over my hand brings me back to present. I realize I am zoning out with a dazed look on my face and a huge lump growing on my head.

Why can't life stay simple? Why can't I be that kid learning to drive with her grandmom forever? Sighing, I turn the key back to off, and climb out.

The bike I want is wedged between the cart and a lawn mower that looks like it might disintegrate any minute. I move the lawn-mower, right the bike and wheel it out of the garage. It's a five-speed mountain bike with disc brakes.

I took it over a few years ago when David said it was too small for him. I like the way it rides over everything, even down steps. It's electric blue with a yellow *Gannondale* signature on the frame. You can tell it's a boy's bike because the middle of the frame is straight across where a girl's bike would dip down.

I wipe the cobwebs off with my bare hands and put air in the tires.

Uncle Leo leans out the back door as I throw my leg over the top tube. "Have a good ride, Rising Star. Talk to you later!"

My stomach does a flip-flop and my spirit tries to hide in the deepest recesses of my mind or heart or ...wherever. I wave back managing a fake smile, then pedal fast down the driveway onto the street towards momentary freedom and... the culdesac where Sofia supposedly lives.

It is a nice morning like most mornings in the North Carolina mountains in summer. Hard to believe the water is so polluted we need a water substitute. Hard to believe there are wildfires in California, earthquakes in Iran, floods in Texas, and I personally just escaped a level four hurricane. Hard to believe but true.

I shake my head and breathe sweet summer air in through my nose and out through my mouth. Layers of softly curved dark green and purple mountains surround the neighborhood; the shape is like a woman lying on her side.

Gold and orange butterflies, green blue hummingbirds and yellow bees are out in full force pollenating flowers in their different styles- wafty, sprinty and steady. I love riding a bike. It is the closest a girl can get to flying.

Soon my stomach settles and I forget about Wüter and extreme weather for now. Maybe Sofia will have a bike and we can ride together. That would be cool. Focusing on positive thoughts and wearing my most determined face, I pedal rotation by rotation to my destination.

The turquoise house with the wraparound porch and wild lawn totally jump out at me when I enter the culdesac. Just like Mom said, impossible to miss.

I dismount and lean my bike against the wooden fence. It is canary yellow and matches the porch. Paint is chipping off in spots but that doesn't make it any less cheery. I open the gate and look around. The blue grass lawn is past my knees and I almost step in dog doo. Watching my step, I walk up the front steps and knock on the door.

Within seconds the grey dog begins barking its alert bark on the other side. Ruff, one two, ruff, one two, ruff, one two.

Through the screen and glass doors, I see Sofia walk over. Her hair is pulled up on top of her head in a tight curly bun. She is wearing a blue tee shirt, jean shorts and her feet are bare. Her toenails are painted the exact blue of her shirt. Nice. She opens the glass door and we stand face to face looking at each other through the screen.

"Good boy, Smokey," she tells the grey dog. Smokey sits down wagging his stub tail.

"Hi," she says looking at me with a question on her face. "Hi," I say back. "I'm Lena. I live a few blocks over. Well, I live here in summer anyway."

I look away trying to think of what to say next and come up with, "You came to our house yesterday looking for your dog. My mom says you just moved here and I thought I'd come by and ask if …you wanna ride bikes or something. We're close to the same age."

I shift my weight and shove my hands in my pockets suddenly super self-conscious about my turquoise romper. Maybe I should have changed.

We look at each other through the screen door kind of sizing each other up. She is at least an inch taller than me and looks more mature.

"I'm fifteen. I'll be sixteen December first. What about you?"

"I turned fifteen a month ago, May 11. I was born on Mother's Day which makes me a Taurus sun sign."

"What's a sun sign?" Sofia asks wrinkling her nose and stepping outside, screen door slamming behind her. Smokey manages to slide out behind her and begins sniffing my legs and feet. I pat his head.

Sofia is pretty, closer to two inches taller than me with dark curly hair, deep brown eyes that curve up on the outside, high cheekbones and medium dark skin.

"A sun sign is the astrological sign you were born under. It tells you a lot about your personality and stuff. I mean really you should know your sun, moon, and rising to get a clear picture. The rising sign is actually the most important one to know. America kind of dumbs it down for people. So like, my rising sign is Aquarius, my moon sign is Taurus. Actually, my moon and sun are the exact same degree in Taurus in the third house. My North Node is zero degrees Sagittarius and … there's a lot more. I wonder what your rising and moon are."

"Uh what?" She laughs and I notice her braces match the silver crescent moon ring on her left index finger.

Ooohh! A moon ring! She looks good in silver. I smile hoping she doesn't think I am weird because I know astrology.

"How do you find your moon and rising sign?"

"Online. They have calculators that make it easy. You just need to know the location and time you were born. Exact time matters otherwise it won't work."

"Oh well, maybe we can do that sometime," she shrugs. "I like your romper. Did you ride your bike over in that?"

"Yea," I say, "I probably shoulda changed but... I wanted to get away from the house fast. Nothing bad just..." I trail off looking away towards my bike then down at Smokey.

"I know that how that feels."

"I like your moon ring," I say reaching out for her hand to get a closer look. When I touch her hand a remembrance happens. I can't describe it better than that. I just know that I know her...like before or always or something. When I touch her hand I know she is my star sister, same soul tribe. We look at each other and smile, curious.

"Do you have a bike?" I ask.

"Wait right here," she tells me. "I'll get it and tell Auntie we are going for a ride."

I sit down on the front step to wait. The grass in the yard is super tall and there are dog piles along the fence but the vibrant purple and white wildflowers add a sort of unruly beauty. The trashcans and recycling bins on the side of the house are over full with brown moving boxes stashed behind them.

Three hummingbird feeders hang from the porch rafters and a small handmade birdhouse filled with seed hangs from the lone maple tree in the yard.

In a couple of minutes the back door opens and closes. Sofia walks around the side of the house pushing a red bike that looks way too big for her.

"This is my Aunt's bike. Mine was stolen in Montana," she says. "I loved that bike. It was a dark purple *Beast* racing bike with full suspension. Fit me perfectly. I rode it every day ... until it was stolen."

"That stinks! Do you know who stole it?"

"Honestly, I think it was my Mom," she frowns biting her bottom lip. Then looks hopeful, "But Dad says if he puts $200 away every month for six months he'll be able to buy me a new one for Christmas. That's $1200 total. I have to do chores to earn half of it. Good bikes are expensive ya know?"

I don't really know what anything costs. No one ever tells me but I nod anyway, acting like I know.

"So I'm riding Auntie's bike til then. It's kind of big for me but if I put the seat down, I can manage."

"But why would your Mom steal your bike?" I ask, "That doesn't make any sense." I look at her raising my right eyebrow only. I am good at doing that but save it for special occasions. It's one of my best faces.

"No, It doesn't," Sofia agrees then shrugs. "My Mom does some pretty weird things. I guess that's why we're here."

She unlocks the seat, slides it down several inches, tightens it, and pushes the bike out the front gate with both hands.

"Come on," she calls over her shoulder.

I follow her out. "Do you like it here?" I ask pushing my bike out behind her.

"I don't know yet," Sofia says, "We've only been here a week and we're still unpacking. I mean, I miss my friends in Montana but the mountains here are pretty and the lake is nice."

"Same." I say. I like saying 'same'. It sounds cool. My friend Ally's older sister says 'same' and she is the coolest girl I know, well the only girl I know, in college. "I've been coming here every summer since I was little to stay with my Grandma except this year she's uh dead. So it's just me, my Mom, my brother David... my Dad right now and my Uncle Leo from California...well he's just visiting. They're not fun like my Grandma was. Mom and David are both like glued to their computer screens and my dad and uncle are all business."

I hang my head and scuff my shoe not wanting to think of the Wüter proposition.

"Ya, a house fulla tackies and business executives sounds real fun," Sofia wrinkles her nose in distaste.

"What's a tackie?"

"You know, people who *live* on their technology, like on their computers and phones. People who would rather play video games and text than talk to people face to face. A tacky."

"Oh ya, that. You kinda have an accent with that word. David is definitely a techie. He hardly ever comes out of his room unless there's an ocean nearby. He's addicted to this weird war game."

"Why does he come out if there's an ocean nearby?" Sofia asks.

"Because he surfs. That's the only other thing he likes to do besides play games. Only where we come from, Wrightsville Beach, there's a swimming and surfing ban ...like no one can go in the ocean because of the oil spill right now and who knows how long that will last."

"A surfing ban?"

"Yeah, there was this huge hurricane." I turn to look at her eyes wide a vision of the powerful wind and rain, the big truck on its side, the dirty swirling water, and all the things flying through the air flood right back into my mind. For a moment, I am back in it, a scared girl praying for her life. I shiver. The hair on my arm stands.

A warm breeze and birds chirping bring me back to the present. Sofia is wearing a look of concern.

"You were back in it, weren't you?" she says touching my arm.

I nod. "It was pretty intense like...my Dad and I barely escaped!" I shake my head wondering what it looks like down there now.

"I saw some of it on the news. Sorry you were in that. It must have been scary..."

We stand in the middle of the street in silence for like thirty seconds. Smokey whines at us from the yard and we start walking again pushing the bikes in front of us.

"So... what about your mom? Why is she on the computer all the time?"

I take a deep breath. "My mom is writing a book so that's her excuse. Well, it's not really an excuse. *It's her job.* She published a book two years ago and it made the *New York Times Best Seller List* and we well...she made a lot of money. She writes romances. They're kinda creepy I think but people love 'em. She needs to publish another book this year while her name is still fresh in reader's minds her agent says. Her agent is this real pushy woman named Cheryl."

"Oh, well that's cool then. Good for her."

"Ya, I'm proud of her and all, it's just writing takes up like all her time now... and she's a lot more serious. It's like all she thinks about it getting published again."

I glance sideways at Sofia. "You ready to ride?"

"Always," says Sofia mounting big red. Her aunt must be a giant. Sofia's toes barely reach the ground but she looks confident. She pushes off and begins pedaling. "Let's go!"

"Gosh your aunt must have long legs," I say. "She does. She's six foot one."

"Wow!"

"My entire family is tall," Sofia says.

Sofia is not wearing a helmet and neither am I.

That means we are both rebels or maybe we just like the wind in our hair. Can you be a responsible rebel? I think so. Either way, I like this girl!

Sofia, already at the end of the street turns and yells over her shoulder, "What are you waiting for?"

I stand and pedal, fast and hard to catch up, my turquoise romper flying up in all sorts of impractical ways. During our two-hour ride, I make sure to find a lot of steps to ride down to show Sofia how bouncy the Gannondale's shocks are. I ride down the library steps, the post-office steps, and down and up some pretty high curbs. She seems impressed but doesn't say so.

We ride our bikes until the sun is directly above our heads and I start to wilt. I realize I haven't eaten anything today because Dad and Uncle Leo ambushed me.

"I need to eat," I say. "I'm getting dizzy. I skipped breakfast today which I never do."

"I'm hungry too plus I should check in with my aunt. Can you come by after dinner? I wanna show you something."

"Ok. You're pretty good on that bike even if it is a little big for you."

It was true. Even on her Aunt's bike Sofia is a stronger uphill rider then me. I am a strong rider and fast downhill and cross-country but had a hard time pacing with her on the up-hills.

"It's because in Montana there are a lot of steep hills to climb and then you fly downhill superfast like a roller coaster. My friends and I used to ride every weekend. We had *fu-un*," Sofia laughs emphasizing the word fun.

"Nice!" I say, stomach growling. I turn my bike due north, the direction of Daffodil House and start pedaling. "See ya after dinner then so you can show me... whatever!" I yell halfway down the street already thinking about food.

"See ya later!" Sofia yells back.

SIXTEEN

Daffodil House kitchen is cool and inviting after my long, hot bike ride. It's also void of family members for which I am grateful. Pouring myself a glass of iced tea first, I then make a ham and swiss sandwich, slicing half a cucumber, half a tomato and adding a little sea salt. I eat the cucumber and tomato first before biting into my sandwich. I am ravenously hungry.

Everything tastes super delicious and I wonder what Sofia is having for lunch. For some reason her face floats into my mind. I see her dark brown eyes and curly hair. The image is crystal clear. She is trying to tell me something. Her mouth moves but I can't hear what she is saying.

"I said, I am having bologna and cheese with mustard," she mouths again with no voice in my mind. The vision is clear and now I understand the message.

I shake my head. I probably got too much sun and need a nap. This sounds logical and logic is my comfort zone plus I want a nap anyway. So, I clean up my few dishes and head upstairs.

Still sweaty from the bike ride I peal off sticky clothes and

pull on a clean pair of soft shorts and tee shirt for my catnap and jump into bed. What a difference a few hours can make. I have a friend now so the world is my oyster. Whatever that means, I think it means I am happy.

WHEN I WAKE UP, it's dark. Clock says 9:01. What in the world? How did I sleep that long? Wow and Mom didn't even wake me for dinner?

Out the window, a perfect sliver crescent moon hangs in the sky and one very bright planet accompanies it. I feel disoriented and disappointed because I didn't go to Sofia's after dinner like I promised. I wonder what planet that is too and make a mental note to research it.

If I went to Sofia's now, I would only be three hours late but it is dark and Mom would not approve. That means I would have to sneak out. What if Sofia is not home or is in bed already. My brain, beginning to weigh options, realizes it is a risky plan at best. I don't have her number so I can't call or text. Then a crazy idea pops into my head. I will think about her really hard and see if I can bring her face into my mind again to talk. Maybe she really did have bologna and cheese for lunch.

Intuition tells me I'm on the right track with this.

I close my eyes.

"Sofia," I say quietly concentrating on my memory of her face, "I need to tell you something."

In that place behind my eyes, black space begins to shift and swirl. Out of the darkness light begins to take shape and form. I watch quietly knowing somehow that this is an old skill, one I mastered lifetimes ago.

Just as I am beginning to see the outline of her face in my mind, Mom knocks on my door.

"Honey, do you feel okay? Are you talking to someone?" She asks poking her head into my dark room.

"I'm okay…but why did you let me sleep through dinner?" I ask in a slightly accusing tone turning on the light.

"I tried to wake you. You would not budge," Mom says sitting on the edge of my bed looking concerned.

"That is *weird,*" I say looking concerned back. "I mean all I did was ride bikes with Sofia all morning. It was hot but I felt fine. Then I came home, had lunch and took a nap. I only meant to sleep for like twenty minutes. It sucks 'cause I promised Sofia I would meet her after dinner. She wanted to show me something."

I hang my head and bite my lip hoping Sofia won't think I didn't show on purpose.

"That's great!" Mom practically yells in my face. "I mean it's great that you met and spent time together. Do you like her? Think you will be friends?" Mom's huge smile makes her eyes light up. Her delight at my having a friend has totally replaced the forehead wrinkly look of concern she wore a few seconds ago.

I laugh at the transformation. She looks pretty and young now. We hug.

"I do. I really like her. I kind of feel like we already are friends and I'm grateful for that."

I jump out of bed, stretching my arms high then swan dive into a forward fold, touching my hands to my feet. Then I stand tall again looking serious and straight at Mom.

"But like why would I sleep so long? I don't like not knowing."

Mom shakes her head slowly looking around like she's searching for an answer somewhere in my room. Her shoulders move up and down in a shrug. "Your body probably needed the sleep. I wouldn't think too much about it. You are a growing girl. You got a lot of sun today and …you did just survive a hurricane. You are under stress. Those things add up!"

I nod in acceptance of Mom's theory.

She stands and hugs me again. "Are you hungry? I saved dinner for you. Chicken and broccoli and sweet potato fries, which I know you love."

"Ooh sweet potato fries. Yay!" I clap turning my little desk lamp on. I pull out the swivel chair and sit down at the old wooden roller desk with little rosebud detail carving around the edges that always makes me feel like I am in the 19th century. I flip open my laptop, fluff my hair and maestro crack my knuckles. "But first...a little research!"

"What are you researching? You know I loooove research," Mom leans in behind me waiting for me to type. I cover the screen with my hands then turn around and cover her eyes.

"Oh, come on, I can't see?" Mom asks all offended sad.

She might be a worrywart workaholic but I would rather her be that than an addict bike thief like Sofia's Mom.

"Kidding!" I say starting to type 'mental telepathy.' "I'm just researching some thingggsss...like mental telepathy and um special gifts being passed down through ancestry."

"Interesting! Are you researching those thingggsss for a reason?" Mom asks emphasizing the word things like I did.

"I'm just keeping myself occupied so I don't freak out over the whole water situation," I shrug. "Maybe I'll write a book like you one day. We'll see..."

"Good idea. Keep yourself busy. That's all we can do sometimes. Let me know how it goes," Mom smoothes my hair. "Your hair gets so light in the summer, Lena. So pretty... and you got some color on your face and shoulders today. Did you wear sunscreen?"

"Yes, Mom."

"Good. If you wear sunscreen now you won't get wrinkles before forty."

"I know, Mom. I'm wearing it."

"I leave you to your research then." Mom bows low like I'm a queen. "Hope to meet your new friend soon. Bring her over anytime. You girls can have a sleep over or camp in the yard if you want. When I was your age my best friend, Diane and I did that all the time. One summer, we camped in the yard so many nights in a row, the grass stopped growing under our tent," she laughs.

Mom's laugh takes me by surprise and all of a sudden I don't want her to leave. I wanna keep her talking. I hardly ever get this mom anymore. Happy, engaged Mom.

"The grass stopped growing? That is so funny!"

Mom smiles and kisses the top of my head. "Oh, before I forget, your father and Uncle Leo went to a pre-market investors dinner in Raleigh. They're spending the night down there."

Mom pauses to touch her earring and fluff her hair. "Have you decided to do the commercial... or the news brief ... or whatever it is Friday?"

I close my laptop and drop my forehead on it with dramatic flair, covering the back of my head with my hands.

"Uuuuhhhh!" I groan. "I guess so. I mean, I wanna make Dad happy *and* I wanna be an actress... but a water substitute is scary, Mom! Humans are like 70% water! If we drink a water substitute won't that make us sub-human?"

I turn my head enough to peep through my arms at Mom.

"I agree with you," Mom says biting her bottom lip and straightening her shirt. "But your father thinks it's too late. Pure water will eventually be ... nearly impossible to get a hold of...and your father's investment... this Wüter... could be the next best thing. The new silver as far as investments go..." Mom's smile has weakened to barely upturned at the corners.

"It's not just about money, Mom," I say softly, sour.

"I know honey," she says backing out my bedroom door. "I have dinner wrapped for you in the fridge. Good night."

Too much reality for Mom.

I stare at the floor for a minute silently praying about the state of Earth, about extreme weather, water scarcity, pollution, consumerism and ask how I can help.

Then I flip my laptop back up and dive into my research. I cannot find a thing about special gifts being passed down through ancestry. I do learn about mental telepathy though.

This is what I find:

"A relaxed, meditative state increases a person's ability to communicate telepathically. Open mindedness enhances the chances of telepathic communications; a closed mind is less likely to be able to transmit or receive effectively. Good health is important too. Everything is weaker when you are weak or sick, including the ability to project thoughts. Some people can communicate telepathically in dreams. Clairvoyance is the term given to a message received in visual form. Hearing an inner

voice is referred to as clairaudience. Claircognizance is a clear intuitive knowing."

I also find that the bright planet next to the moon this month is Venus. I close my laptop partially satisfied with the research findings and head downstairs to eat.

SEVENTEEN

Next morning I high tail it over to Sofia's house and pound on the front door. A tall woman in pink pajamas answers with a worried look on her face and a coffee mug in her hand.

"I thought you were the police pounding on the door like that. Is everything ok?" Her eyes narrow, "Are you selling some- thing?" She looks me up and down.

"No, I'm uh I'm Sofia's friend. I was supposed to come over last night but I fell asleep and I, I want to apologize." I blurt out embarrassed looking at my feet. Then, "sorry I knocked so hard." I shrug and smile sheepishly.

"Oh," she says looking relieved. "You're the girl she rode bikes with yesterday?"

I nod.

"Sofia!" she yells into the house. "Your friend is here!"

Sofia appears behind her momentarily in jean shorts and a tee shirt. Pink pajama lady, I assume her aunt, recedes back into the house.

"Hey," Sofia says. "So, you fell asleep, huh?" "Ya until nine! Sorry! It was so weird."

"Don't worry about it. I did too. I thought maybe I was getting sick or something but I feel fine. Wanna come in?"

"Yes, please."

"Don't mind the mess, ok? We haven't finished unpacking." I follow her in, closing the door behind me.

The house smells like dog, coffee, cigarette smoke and bacon. We walk through a nice sized living room with a stone fire- place. In the fireplace, a stack of wood sits expertly positioned on a metal grate. A chestnut brown leather couch and matching easy chair with a towel on it, for the dog I assume, look pleasantly used and comfortable. There is a floor lamp with a Native American hunt scene on the shade, a small table, and an easy chair. On the couch a Puff the Magic Dragon stuffed animal sits guarding several Dr. Seuss books.

Sofia leads me through the dining room stacked with boxes and then through a neat and clean kitchen. Towards the last room on the first floor, the family room, the sound of a laughing, clap- ping TV audience and the scent of cigarette smoke get stronger.

Toys are scattered across the floor in the family room, which is sunken and carpeted. There is a large screen TV, a couch, and a coffee table. Pink pajama lady is watching a morning talk show folding laundry and smoking a cigarette. Gosh, I didn't think anyone smoked cigarettes in the house anymore.

"Aunt Laurie, this is my new friend Lena. She spends summers here but she's from a beach where you can't drink the water or swim in the ocean anymore because the water is too polluted. Lena, this is Aunt Laurie. She's from Montana like me."

Aunt Laurie, tall and skinny with bright blue eyes and freckles running over the bridge of her nose, is pretty athletic for a smoker. Like she played basketball and volleyball in college or something. Her hair, light brown and wavy, not curly like Sofia and her sisters, is pulled back in a ponytail. She looks about twenty-five.

Aunt Laurie's smile turns into a frown at the introduction. Putting her cigarette down, she reaches over the back of the couch to shake my hand. I grab hold of it firmly and pump once, twice, giving it a good squeeze so she knows I am trust- worthy and not a push over. I read a book on body language once and you wouldn't believe the things you can tell from a handshake.

She laughs. "I like a girl with a strong handshake. You'll make a fine politician one day, Lena. Uh what beach are you from again?"

"Wrightsville Beach."

"Ohhhh," she cringes making an O and squinting her eyes, "where the hurricane was, right?"

"Yeah," I say sad. "We were in that hurricane, my dad and I. We like barely escaped."

"Oh my Lord!" Aunt Laurie shakes her head vigorously,

exhaling sharply. "It's hard tellin' what'll happen with the weather anymore. Glad you're ok."

"Thanks. Me too."

Sofia and I exchange glances.

"Was there a lot of damage to your house?" Aunt Laurie asks taking a long pull on her cigarette.

"Uh I don't know we haven't seen it yet. We're kinda staying here for awhile..."

Aunt Laurie nods solemnly. She blows a smoke ring into the air, which hovers like a smelly white halo around her head before dissipating.

"What's this one about?" Sofia asks her aunt nodding towards the TV.

"Oh, it's another one about family's reuniting," Aunt Laurie says picking up a blue towel to fold and add to the pile. "You know I am a sucker for that."

Sofia snorts a laugh at her Aunt. Then to me, "Ready to see my room?"

"Yep."

We walk back through the kitchen and dining room, up the stairs to the second floor.

"Where's your little sister?" I ask at the top of the stairs. "How do you know I have a little sister?" Sofia's forehead wrinkles. "I haven't mentioned her yet."

Four closed brown wooden doors line the upstairs hall, which is decorated with Native American art. We walk to the last door. It has a small gold 'S' in the center. Sofia pushes it open.

"The day you came over looking for Smokey, I came looking for you. I nearly tripped over your sister and her friend drawing on someone's driveway a few houses down on my street. She looks like you. Same hair and all," I say. "Did she ever give you the message?"

"What message?"

"I told her to tell you to come back to our house, er uh to the place you found Smokey.

"Naw, she didn't tell me. She's only five ya know plus she's hardly ever home. She has a best friend on your street and they are like inseparable."

"But you just moved here. How does she have a best friend?"

"My dad knows a guy here. His friend is her dad. He got my Dad the job before we moved. I mean Tab, my sister, and his daughter just met but ... you know, little kids make friends fast," Sofia shrugs. "They'll be in the same kindergarten class."

"Oh, well, that's good."

Sofia's room smells better than the rest of the house even though the dog is in there asleep on the floor. He looks up when we walk in but stays where he is.

"And this," says Sofia pointing to the dog, "is Smokey."

"Gees, there's more Smokey in here than the rest of the house, haha," I laugh doofily at my own joke. "Get it?"

"Omygosh, girl. You gotta work on your skills," Sofia says rolling her eyes. "Ya, I get it."

Sofia sits on the floor next to the dog and pets his head. He puts his chin on her knees.

"I believe you've met Lena, Smokey, but have not been officially introduced," she says.

I sit down too.

He looks at me and wags his grey stub tail. I pet his back and ears.

He gives me his paw.

"Smokey is a Weimaraner and needs to run a lot. We had land in Montana... over a hundred acres and now all he has is this tiny yard. He's got loose twice already. Once he ended up at your house. That's probably the day you met my sister."

Smokey's short, grey fur is super-soft and he has very large, light sage green eyes.

"I think he is depressed 'caus he's cooped up with nowhere to run. He sleeps a lot more than he used to," Sofia says.

I look around. Sofia's room is smaller than mine but I like the way it's decorated. Her bed is made and covered in sea green blankets with a matching canopy. There is one stuffed animal in front of many white and cream-colored pillows, a teal sea horse. A white desk fitting perfectly under the only window in the room shows a great view of the mountains. The window is open and white lace curtains move gently in the breeze.

A white bookshelf connected to her desk has books and framed pictures on it. An old doll sits in a jean colored beanbag chair next to a brush, comb and other hair things. There is a vintage vanity with a large oval mirror attached to it and a roller stool with a denim cloth cover. The cream-colored ceiling fan is on full speed and a plastic green feather hangs down in the center for a pull chain. The fan makes a whirring noise that is relaxing.

Smokey rolls on his side and stretches out pushing against my knees a little with the pads of his paws.

"So um...what did you want to show me?"

"I wanted to show you a book I found," Sofia says, "about elemental vortexes in these mountains." She crawls over to her bookshelf on hands and knees and pulls off a book lying on top of the other books. Smokey opens an eye.

"Elemental vortexes?" I say raising my eyebrows and swiveling my head around like a night owl. "You mean like earth, air, fire, water, and space?"

"Yep."

"I was totally welcoming ... I mean *thinking* about the elements this week. Interested, for sure."

"I thought you would be," she says passing me the book.

It is an old book with the words, *Sleeping Lady Mountain Magic: Elemental Vortexes* written on the front of a dark blue leather cover. Bound my hand, there is a row of symbols underneath the title that I can barely make out: triangles, circles, squares, squiggly lines and swirls like some kind of alien language.

"Cool!" I exclaim, opening it right up to the middle where there is a map.

"Does Sleeping Lady mean these mountains?" I ask pointing out the window.

"I think so," she nods. It looks like a lady sleeping on her side, don'tcha think?"

"I've always thought that," I say breathless and dizzy all of a sudden. "Let me ask you something super serious." I straighten up, put the book down, and twist a strand of hair around my finger. "What did you have for lunch yesterday?"

Sofia's brown eyes widen then she slaps her leg and laughs, "Ha ha! That's super serious? Bologna and cheese with mustard. It's my favorite," she says making a wide-eyed funny face and rubbing her belly. "Why?"

"Oh my gosh, this is getting weird," goose bumps form on my arms and legs. Smokey sits up in tune with the energy in the room, inquisitive. "You are not going to believe this but I knew that."

"What do you mean?" Sofia asks making a hurt feelings face. "Don't go all smoke and mirrors on me. I am just showing you a book I found."

"Wait. What?"

I cover my face with my hands and shake my head confused by her reaction. Then I realize she thinks I am making fun of her because of the vortex book.

"Sofia. This has nothing to do with the book. I am not making fun of you or it. I am totally serious! I really saw your face and you really told me what you had for lunch when I asked you yesterday in my mind." I return wide-eyed jumping a little for emphasis with my best and most serious, 'ya gotta trust me' look.

Sofia stares at me with narrowed eyes, trying to decide whether or not to believe me, I guess.

"I researched mental telepathy last night because of that ... and ... other reasons ...and I ... I found that it's much easier to do when you're relaxed and open minded. When you get an image in your mind that's called clairvoyance and when you hear a message it's clairaudience. If you totally just know something, that's claircognizance."

"Okay." Sofia says. "Where are you going with this?"

Smokey looks at us curious then turns around several times to find a perfect spot. He licks my hand before lying back down reassuringly. He knows I am telling the truth.

"He likes you," Sofia says. "He never licks anyone, only me.

Dad says he is a good judge of character."

We look at Smokey then at each other. "So, do you believe me?" I ask feeling like this very moment might make or break our friendship.

Sofia nods, "I believe you." I let out a deep exhale. I didn't realize I was holding my breath.

"Wanna try it now?" she asks shrugging her shoulders. "To see if you can do it again, I mean... if *we* can do it?" She scratches a mosquito bite on her long, brown leg

"Do you have an aloe plant?" I ask.

"What," Sofia looks confused? "An aloe plant?"

"Yeah, my grandma used to put aloe on mosquito bites to help them heal faster. It's good for taking the inflammation down and they itch less."

"Thank you, nurse Lena," Sofia says rolling her eyes up to the ceiling. "No, we do not have an aloe plant. Now can we please get back to the issue at hand? Do…you…want… to…try… it…now?" Sofia asks again one word at a time very slowly and a little aggressive sounding which I do not appreciate. Then she pulls her legs up under her and sits on her heals. Moving her face close to mine she whispers, "The mind reading thing I mean."

"Ok, fine," I say not sure if I like the idea because what if I can't do it again? I pull my ponytail out, fluff my hair and close my eyes. "Give me a minute to clear my head, please. I wanna give this my best shot."

Once Gram and I watched a funny old talk show called the *Late Show with Johnny Carson* where an old guy mind-read letters people sent him. Before he tried it he would close his eyes and concentrate. It seemed to help.

"No problem," Sofia says closing her eyes too. "I'll follow your lead on this since you came up with it.

I open an eye to see her taking out her ponytail and fluffing

her own brown curly hair. I have to laugh.

She is doing exactly as I am. She opens an eye and giggles, "What?" she asks.

A warm wind stirs the white curtains and sea green canopy bringing a faint cinnamon rose scent with it. It blows our hair around tickling our noses.

Gram.

Best to keep that for another conversation entirely. I squeeze my eyes shut tight, looking at the dark behind them. Right now I need to prove I am telling the truth.

"Gram," I say in my mind, *"if this is the friend er the Star Seed, star sister or whatever you said I'd be friends with forever, please help me read her mind. Thanks."*

I open my eyes and concentrate on Sofia. Her eyes are still closed, long eyelashes curling at the tips over sculpted high cheekbones. Her brown-black, curly hair is loose and wild. She holds her hands on her lap patient, lips pursed in concentration. "I'm ready," I say. "I am going to ask you a question in my mind and you answer me, okay?"

"Yes," she says without moving in a calm, deep voice.

"Sofia, what color is my bike?" I ask her in my mind.

"Blue," she says out loud. Our eyes flutter open. We stare at each other.

"So, you heard my question?"

"I guess so but I answered out loud right?"

I nod. Again a warm breeze flutters the white curtain and green canopy and our hair moves about.

"Let's try again," she says. "This time let me ask." I nod in agreement and close my eyes.

"Lena, what is your sun sign?" comes Sofia's question in my mind.

"I am a Taurus Sun and Moon, and Aquarius Rising," I answer back without speaking.

Sofia gasps grabbing my hands and squeezing hard, "I heard you loud and clear, girl. I don't know what any of that means but I heard you! Have you ever been able to do this before?"

"Only with my Grandma." I admit. Shaking my hands away from her. That girl is strong! "But mind-reading isn't the only strange thing happening right now." I pause scanning her face to see whether I should continue.

Sofia's eyes get wide, "Go on."

I exhale loudly with horse lips because in yoga they tell you that kind of breathing is relaxing. "Okay, so I told you my Grandma died in January, right? The one I could communicate with telepathically like I just said... I mean the *only* other person I ever could...besides you."

Hot tears stream down my face. Soon I am shaking and can't stop. My shoulders convulse like I am being electrocuted and I hide my face in my hands.

"Honey, its ok to share your true feelings with Sofia," Gram's soothing voice comes into my head. *"A similar magic runs in her blood. You are Star Seeds of the same high frequency..."*

Sofia scoots over and puts an arm around me. I cry for what seems like a very long time.

Finally, out of tears, I wipe my wet face with my hands, run my hands through my hair and sit up straight. "Sorry. I didn't know that was coming," I say embarrassed. "I guess I needed it."

"It's totally fine, girl. I don't like crying in front of people either but it feels good to let it out sometimes. Refreshing like summer rain," Sofia goofs making rainfall gesture with her hands over her head and face.

That hits my funny bone in just the right place apparently because pretty soon we are rolling on the floor laughing so loud her aunt comes back to check on us.

"What in the world are you girls doing?" Aunt Laurie asks loudly over our laughter.

"It's okay, Aunty!" snorts Sofia, "We are just laughing at summer rain!"

"Summer rain? It's not raining out." Aunt Laurie scans the room looking for a clue to our laughter. Finding nothing she shakes her head, "Y'all are on the fast track to crazy town," she says smiling and rolling her eyes before closing the door behind her.

"Y'all are on the fast track to crazy town," Sofia mimics her aunt, invisible cigarette in hand." We burst out laughing again and clutch our bellies until we can barely breathe. Finally, our laughter fades and we sit up.

"Want an iced coffee?" Sofia asks wiping happy tears from her eyes.

"No thanks. I like iced mochas but not plain coffee," I say wrinkling my nose in distaste. "It's so... bitter."

"Not if you put a bunch of milk and sugar in it," Sofia says, "then it's like..." she pauses, "liquid dessert." She makes a googly eyed in-love-with-coffee face and rubs her hands together. Sofia is funny and boy am I glad. I need to laugh.

"Just water, please," I say. "Might as well enjoy it while we can."

"Kay, be right back," she calls halfway to the kitchen already with her long legged stride.

While Sofia is in the kitchen, I have a quick look at myself in the mirror and gasp at how red and blotchy my face is from crying. My hair is kind of knotted on the side too.

"Jees!" I say starting to straighten myself up. I brush my hair with her brush and smooth some of my lip balm on my lips and brows for 'instant polish,' a trick my friend Ally taught me. I look around her room for a face spritz toner but don't see one, so I settle into the beanbag chair and open *Sleeping Lady Mountain Magic: Elemental Vortexes.*

Some of the words are blotted out but most are legible. There are sketches of the elements: Earth, Air, Fire, Water, and Space and maps that show where the local vortexes are for each element.

Is a "vortex" a power spot, black hole, or like a portal to another dimension? I don't exactly know and will have to Google it later to learn the real definition.

"Okay!" Sofia says wider-eyed entering her room drinking her sugar milk iced coffee and handing me a glass of water. "Isn't that a cool book?"

"Yes," I tell her using telepathy. She smiles.

"Haha," she says telepathically back. *"Maybe we are on the fast track to crazy town."*

"Don't start that again," I think back.

Sofia sits down and sips her coffee. It smells good but I am happy with my water and drink it in one long gulp. Ahh! Naturally refreshing.

"Wanna finish telling me about your Grandma now?" she asks absent-mindedly petting Smokey. "I have a Grandma story for you too. I'll tell you after. We'll trade."

For the next several hours Sofia and I talk. I tell her all about Gram, how amazing she was alive and how she came to me recently in spirit and told me I would meet my star sister soon. I tell her how Gram said Sofia and I both have ancestral gifts like telepathy in our blood and how we will be doing some kind of mission together. I tell her how my dream and Gram told me a ritual welcome to Earth's messengers, the elements, would unlock those ancestral gifts. I tell her I did just that and how natural it felt and … how cool is it that she has the element book?! It must all be tied together.

I know it's a lot to take in. It is for me too. But the elemental vortex book and the mental telepathy we share make it a heck of alot easier for me to tell her everything at once. I let it all out like a flood and it feels good. When I'm done, I breathe a deep sigh of relief and melt like a puddle on the floor.

Then Sofia tells me about her Grandma. Grandma Doe, an Eastern Cherokee Native American, who lived to 102 years old!

She was her mother's adopted mother who lived in Idaho. Sofia hardly ever saw her but one summer, when she was twelve, she stayed with her on the reservation. The Eastern Cherokee tribe had a special gathering for her Grandma's 100th birthday that summer.

"It was the most beautiful amazing, exciting thing I have ever experienced," Sofia says glowing just talking about the memory. "Tribe people all ages, brought presents for my Grandma, colorful jewelry, blankets, clothing, cookware, moccasins, bags, rattles, magic things for ceremony and more," Sofia says beginning to weave the story for me.

"There were tents everywhere! Women set up a loom and made sunrise blankets under a tent and there was another tent for children to make dream catchers and another one for ceremonial face painting. The men hunted and grilled deer, wild turkey, and elk. They had an outdoor kitchen and delicious smells of roots, vegetables, meats, herbs, and spices I'll prob- ably never smell again rose high into the summer sky. Everything tasted so good too. They even made candied sage. That stuff is amazing."

"The best thing about it though was the ceremony," Sofia says finishing her coffee with flair and licking her lips.

"The chief wasn't there the entire time. He came the morning of the ceremony and they set up a special tent for him. A lot of sweet smelling smoke came out of it. I wasn't allowed to go near it. Only the men were.

At midnight, the chief came out. He was big like a brown bear and had a huge headdress on. He called to the four directions for their blessings and then to heaven and Earth and finally to the elements. Then he presented my Grandma with a beaded leather necklace with 100 sacred shells on it. I wonder where that necklace is now? The ceremony ended in dancing and singing and lasted until the sun came up. I wish I could show you pictures. It was awesome."

I sit there trying to imagine it. It must be amazing being part of something so important.

"Was your Mom there for any of it?" is the dumbass I thing I decide to ask.

"No." The light in Sofia's eyes immediately dulls and a shadow falls across her face. "She was probably off goofing up somewhere doing whatever a goof up Mom does. I mean I hardly remember when she wasn't messing up. My earliest memories are like when I was four and five, Dad would come home from work, Mom would be passed out asleep on the couch and I would be taking care of myself."

"Oh but your little sister is only five so she must..."

Sofia cuts me off an acid edge to her voice. "She pulled herself together for a year once when my dad threatened to kick her out. Just long enough to have my little sister then started messing up again."

"Wow. I can tell you're mad at her."

"Yes, I am." Sofia crosses her arms across her chest and scowls at the wall.

"Was your mom Native American too? Because you look Native American but if Grandma Doe was your adopted grandmom, where does it come from?"

"I'm a quarter Cherokee. My Mom was Eastern Cherokee Native, on her Mother's side. Her father was African American.

My mom's real mom was apparently a wild woman and didn't want to be tied down with a kid so put my mom up for adoption. The tribe tries to take care of each other so Grandma Doe adopted my mom even though she was like sixty at the time. She had her own house and land but could never have her own kids so it worked out.

But *my* Mom turned out to be wild just like her and gave my Grandma a real hard time. She was beautiful and a talented artist they tell me but barely graduated high school. Then she met my dad. He was working on a construction site... Anyway, we don't need to get into all that..." she trails off.

Smokey is whining.

"He needs to go out," Sofia says. "And I'm getting kinda hungry. What are you doing for lunch?"

We walk into the kitchen, Smokey following at our heels. "We're taking Smokey out!" Sofia yells to her Aunt who is still on the couch watching talk shows.

Sofia attaches a brown leather leash to Smokey's bright orange collar. He pulls her out the door.

Ping. It's Mom texting me. I read it as I close the door behind us.

Mom: *Do you and Sofia want to camp in the yard tonight?*

Me: *I'll ask*

MY MIND IS SWIRLING THINKING of Sofia's life in Montana and Idaho, places I have never been. I can't imagine having a mom who takes pills until she passes out. I want to ask her more but I can see it hurts her. Best to wait and let Sofia bring it up again because I know when I don't want to talk about something no one is gonna make me.

Happy with my decision to keep my mouth shut for now, I look up. Sofia is walking down the street with Smokey who is sniffing things and peeing on people's lawns, probably where other dogs have left their mark.

"Hey, Sofia!" I yell.

"Yeah?" she yells back holding the leash away from her to give Smokey as much space as possible while he hunches over grimacing to poo.

A lady leans out the front door, "You will pick up after your dog, young lady. If you don't have a bag, I have one right here."

Sofia does not have a bag and looks sheepish.

The lady waves a double plastic bag out the door. "If you are going to have a dog in this neighborhood, you need to pick up after it."

"Yes, Ma'am," Sofia says apologetically retrieving the double bag from her.

"And you will put that bag in your own trashcan, thank you." The lady crosses thick arms in front of an enormous chest, her mouth set in a determined, no-nonsense line as Sofia picks up Smokey's steaming poo.

"This is my least favorite part of having a dog," Sofia says under her breath.

"What was that dear?" the lady asks loudly.

"Sorry, Ma'am. We used to have land and I never did the leash and bag thing before. I'll remember to bring one next time I walk him. Thank you!" Sofia says loudly tying the bag in a knot and racing back to her house to toss it in the trashcan, Smokey running alongside.

"Picking up poo stinks literally!" Sofia says dropping the bag into an already full trashcan. Smokey hangs his head.

"Oh it's not your fault, bud. We'll get out into those mountains tomorrow so you can run off leash and poo wherever you want, I promise." She pats his head and he looks hopeful.

"What did you want, Lena?" she turns to me hands on hips still irritated from the leash and bag thing.

"Oh, ah my mom invited you over. She says we can camp in the yard tonight if we want. We have a pretty big tent I can set up and it's fenced in so we're safe. Maybe you can bring the book."

"I'll ask my Dad, he gets home from work around six and then we eat. I can probably come over after that. He likes to know who I'm hanging out with and where they live. You know." She shrugs. "Text me so I have your number. I mean not that we have to text."

She rolls her eyes and claps a hand on my shoulder.

"Let's promise not to tell anyone we can communicate telepathically, uh with our minds, okay? They might make us perform on talk shows and stuff. I have a feeling my Aunty would drive us to the first TV studio who would put us on."

"Ya. It's our gift and no one needs to know about it but us," I agree.

We shake on it.

Sofia tells me her number and I shoot her a quick text.

'Lena.'

"OK, well, see you tonight, I hope."

I swing a leg over my bike and wave. Sofia waves back and I pedal away towards Daffodil House. Trees, cars, homes, and lawns fly past me as I turn recent events over in my mind. I can hardly believe how fast life can change once things start to happen. I have got to write in to Kiki Astromatrix.

EIGHTEEN

Approaching Daffodil House on full alert, part of me wants to avoid Uncle Leo and Dad another day hoping for a miracle. Maybe they'll change their minds about investing in a water cleanup or ask me to do a commercial for shampoo or shoes instead. Dad's truck is not out front so maybe I am in luck.

I park my bike in the garage, steal into the kitchen quiet as a mouse, and pour myself some monitored water. A cream-colored envelope with my name on it, leans against the vase of roses on the kitchen table. I open it. A folded piece of paper flutters to the floor.

For our rising star,

We're flying you first class! See you Friday at LAX.

-Love, Management

Ohmygosh! Dad and Uncle Leo didn't even wait for my

answer. I bend down and open the piece of paper. It's a first-class flight itinerary from RDU to LAX. The decision's been made.

"Mom!" I yell as loud as I can. "Motherrrr!!"

Leaving the letter and itinerary on the table, I dart upstairs. Mom is, of course, at her desk. Her door is open and she is wearing the headphones.

"Mother!" I say loudly hands flexed in annoyance like I'm about to pop an invisible beach ball.

"Yes?" Mom asks turning towards me, sliding the headphones down and craning her neck like a turtle.

"Dad and Uncle Leo bought me a ticket before I gave them an answer! Did you know that?"

"Would you rather them give the commercial to someone else?" Mom leans back in her swivel chair, taking her glasses off and rubbing her eyes.

"That is not the point!" I say stamping my foot and scowling. "I just wish it was for something else! I don't wanna promote a water substitute. I want water to be clean!"

Suddenly feeling the weight of the world on my shoulders, I literally cannot stand upright anymore. Melting like a wax candle onto the floor, I curl into child's pose then crawl over to Mom's legs, leaning my head on her lap.

She pets my head.

"These are confusing times, hon. People everywhere, even adults, are confused," she sighs and clears her throat. "Let's take a minute and look at the facts together. Okay? Facts always make you feel better."

I whimper softly and nod.

"One you will make money. Two when you turn eighteen, you can use the money for whatever you want. Three you can put some of it towards a clean water project if that's what you want. And four, because it's the number of angels," Mom says stroking my hair, "You will gain exposure as an *actress* which is something you've always dreamed of."

I whimper and sniffle like a fifteen-year old baby, listening to

Mom logic.

"Your father and Uncle Leo think this thing is gonna be big, this Wüter... and I've never known them to be wrong where investments are concerned." Mom drums my head softly with her fingertips. "Again, it's a great way for you to get into the family business the way you want. You have to look at the glass half full."

"Omygosh Mom, the glass half full? Of what ... a water substitute?" I push away from her instantly angry again and sit cross- legged just out of her reach. I look at her accusingly.

"Lena," Mom says quietly turning to face me in her swivel chair. "I'm just lining up the facts for you because you're upset and I don't want you to miss out on a great opportunity."

"So, you're saying ... if I do this commercial, I can do what I want with the money *when* I am 18 and maybe help clean up water if there is water to clean up in three years." I verify pulling at a string on the antique Tabriz carpet, twisting it around my middle finger. I watch Mom wince as I do it. It's an expensive rug, a one of a kind but she doesn't challenge me which appeases me... a tiny bit.

"But can I even *trust* Dad and Uncle Leo to let me do what I want with the money? I mean ...what if they have it all planned out for me, the investments and stuff?"

"Well, I guess that's a risk you'll have to take. It's either that or sit on the sideline, watch someone take the part, and do nothing."

"Ahhhh!" I shout like a banshee banging my hands on the

antique carpet. A tiny cloud of dust plumes up and the carpet string snaps and dangles from my finger.

"What's with all the noise, dorkweed?" David's lanky frame appears in the doorway. "Why are you yelling?"

"Your sister is going to Los Angeles Friday to be in a commercial ...and she is excited," Mom explains in a matter of fact manner, keeping a check on energy level in the room.

"What for one of Uncle Leo's jams?"

I nod and stand up. "Dad's gonna be there too. It's for a water substitute."

"A water *substitute*?" my shirtless man bun wearing brother curls his top lip, confused. "Did he leave yet?"

"Yes, he and Leo are on the way to RDU now. Your father wants to make this special for Lena. She'll have her own dressing room, a makeup artist, hair stylist... everything," Mom smiles. "I think it's cute."

"Did he say that?" I ask getting sucked in to glamour faster than a spider in a vacuum. "But, wait. If they went to a conference yesterday, did they even come back this morning or ...omygosh they bought my ticket before they left, didn't they?"

Mom purses her lips and raises her eyebrows.

"So I never had a choice. Why did they even ask me then?" "Ask you what? Do I get a choice?" David interrupts waving me out of the way to stand behind Mom and rub her shoulders. "Ahhh, Mom. There's good surf in LA. Can I go too? I might not get another chance to surf for awhile."

"Eeee," Mom squeals under my brother's hands. "I didn't know how sore my shoulders were... you're pretty good at that."

"Can I go too?" my brother persists.

"I'm sorry David, this is a business trip for your sister only.

It's her first paid acting job and we don't want to take any of that away from her."

"Awww, that's not fair..." David howls immediately removing his massaging hands away from Mom's shoulders. "When am I gonna get to surf again?"

"How are your studies coming?" Mom counters.

I exit quickly leaving them to a private debate, jaw set. Mom's right though, I either play or sit on the sideline. When I have my own money I can do more good.

AS SOON AS I get to my room, I put my laptop on the floor and lay down in front of it. I study and read this way a lot, on my stomach propped up on my arms. Sitting too long hurts my neck and back.

I say a silent prayer before opening the computer, asking how I can help Earth and all beings with this commercial opportunity and not just be selfish. Then I Gogle the latest Kiki Astromatrix YouTube video. She hasn't posted anything since the *Uranus in Taurus* video so I go to that one and comment.

"Kiki! I am writing to tell you about the changes you predicted! On Saturday afternoon I barely escaped a hurricane with my father. We were in that one at Wrightsville Beach. Now we're in the mountains. Yesterday, I made a new friend, and today, Tuesday I got my first acting job. I am flying to Los Angeles Friday to do it. So many changes I can hardly keep up. Thanks for keeping us informed! I don't know what I would do without you!" (Lena 15)

Ping. A text from Sofia.

"Be over at 8 with book."

"OK," I text back, and scroll through the rest of my messages. There are several from Sierra and Naia, a few from other friends at school. But I don't respond to any of them.

I was gonna research something else, what was it? Oh, yeah, vortexes.

There is a ton of information on vortexes. Here are the three definitions I find most relevant.

1. *A vortex is a place in nature where the Earth is exceptionally alive and healthy... where there is tremendous natural beauty created by the elements of land, light, air, and water.*
2. *A vortex is a place on the planet with increased energy. The energy of a vortex acts as an amplifier... When we are in a vortex the energy will amplify or magnify what we bring it.*
3. *For certain people, vortexes are entryways into other dimensions.*

AT 8:01PM a knock on the front door. I run downstairs to open it and the most handsome man I ever saw is standing next to Sofia, one strong, tan arm slung around her shoulders. With perfect posture and broad chest tapering to a slim waist, you can tell he is or was an athlete. He is wearing sneakers, tan shorts, and a sage green polo shirt.

This is Sofia's Dad? I am staring.

"Hi Lena! This is my Dad. Dad this is my new friend, Lena. She lives here in the summer. This was her Grandparents' house."

"This house is a great color," Sofia's dad says flashing a genuinely happy smile.

Mom walks up from behind me and shakes his hand.

"Hi, I'm Doreen, Lena's mom. My father painted this house the color of my favorite flower, the daffodil, when I was nine. We've had it repainted a half dozen times over the years to keep it just that shade of yellow."

"I'm Joe," says Sofia's Dad.

His arm muscles move like a fine-tuned machine as he shakes Mom's hand. He has the same dark eyes as Sofia's with long eyelashes that curl at the tip. His hair is light brown and wavy like his sister's. He is about six foot five.

I stand with my arms behind my back rocking back and forth, heel to toe, heel to toe, suddenly shy.

"Your dad is cuuute!" I think at Sofia.

"All my friends say that," she thinks back rolling her eyes.

"The girls are going to camp in the back yard tonight. It's fenced in and I'll be here all night so they'll be fine." Mom says. "I used to do it when I was a kid. One summer my friend Diane and I camped back there so many nights in a row the grass stopped growing under our tent."

Sofia's Dad laughs. I lean into Mom.

If they only knew how many times I've heard that story! "Sounds like a great idea," he says. His eyes squint into a smile revealing a dimple in one cheek.

Ok, that's too much. He is officially not cute now. The dimple is just overboard. I regain my composure immediately, grabbing Sofia loosely by the wrist, and begin pulling her inside in slow motion.

The parents laugh.

Joe takes off his baseball cap before kissing his daughter on the forehead. "Have fun tonight Sof. Call if you need anything."

"I will Dad," Sofia says wrangling out of my grasp to slip her slim arms around her father's tree trunk of a neck. She gives him a quick hug pressing her cheek to his. Straightening, he replaces his trucker style cap high and to the right and steps off the front porch.

"Nice to meet you ladies. I am glad Sofia has a friend in the neighborhood."

NINETEEN

At 11:11PM Sofia and I are 'glamping' or glamorous camping, in a green five-person tent in the back yard. We have blankets, sleeping bags, and pillows cushioning the floor like it's Cleopatra's lair or something. A rechargeable plastic lantern, and ball glass jars with lids full of lavender lemonade stick up out of the cushy floor cloud.

No moon in the sky tonight but trillions of stars and Venus shine through the clear plastic moon roof of the tent. The tent flaps are open for fresh air and we are relaxing, enjoying the night when Sofia pulls *Sleeping Lady Mountain Magic: Elemental Vortexes* out of her backpack.

"There is something special about this book," she says placing the book on her lap and opening it to the first page. "I have no idea why but I feel connected to it somehow."

I lean over and touch the blue leather cover.

"Oh, before I forget, I researched what vortex means," I say reaching into my shorts pocket for the folded up piece of paper.

"I found a ton of information," I wave the paper around, "but these three here make the most sense with your book and the maps in it and all."

"You actually wrote them down on a piece of paper with a pen?" Sofia says amazed, "You are awesome."

"Thanks, I try."

"I don't even have a pen and paper in my room, right now. We might have one or two in the kitchen. I should get one...for my room. I do everything on my laptop and phone," she frowns. "Gosh, pen and paper is so old school...but like way cooler."

"Did you wanna hear the definition?" I interrupt.

"Oh, this is the part where I stop talking and listen?" Sofia giggles putting her hand over her mouth.

"Ya," I nod wide eyed in the dark switching the lantern on to read. "So...as we know the Earth is a living organism." I spread my hands wide gesturing towards our surroundings, the actress in me coming out. "A vortex then ... is a place in nature where the Earth is exceptionally alive and healthy. In a vortex the health of living Earth is reflected in a tremendous natural beauty created by the elements of land, light, air, and water. That definition is by a guy named Mr. Sedona. My grandma says space is the fifth element but he doesn't include space. The book has space too right?"

Sofia nods keeping her hand over her mouth.

"So that was number one. Number two, a vortex is a place on the planet with increased energy. The energy of a vortex acts as an amplifier. When we are in a vortex the energy will amplify or magnify what we bring it. And the third and final definition is...for certain people, vortexes are entryways into other realms and dimensions."

"Girl!" Sofia exclaims flinging her hands away from her mouth like a geyser erupting. "My arm hairs are standing up! Dude, an entryway into other dimensions? Hells yeah! That one feels right!" Sofia's dark eyes look huge by the gleam of the lantern; almost otherworldly.

I fold the paper, put it back in my pocket, and put the lantern down between us. My arms hairs are standing up too and I shiver even though it's warm out, "Where did you get that book again?"

"I found it the day we moved in... on a bookshelf in my room. It was like the only thing left in the entire house. And honestly, I was gonna throw it away but it would not leave my hand. Like literally I could not throw it away. Then I was so busy unpacking and putting my room together I forgot about it until I met you I haven't even read it all the way through yet.

But now," she says tracing a hand-written word with her fingers, "I feel like it belongs to me. Like I didn't just *find it* by accident you know? Like it was put there *for me to find*. I know that sounds weird but it's not weird in a scary way. It's weird in a *good* way," she sighs. "I can't explain it any better than that."

A warm breeze and the scent of cinnamon and rose enter the tent.

Gram.

Before I can respond to Sofia, Gram begins speaking in my mind.

"Tonight is the Aquarius New Moon, a very good night for beginnings."

"Talk about being weird in a good way! I know exactly what you mean!" I exclaim rubbing my face with both hands and looking skyward.

I was not expecting Gram to show tonight but then I guess I don't know what to expect with anything anymore. Making a mental note to get used to clairaudience and clairvoyance so I don't lose my cool someplace in public or whatever, I sit up straight, fluff my hair, and clear my throat.

"Uhhh so remember how I told you my Grandma speaks to me in my mind sometimes like you and I can speak to each other telepathically ... you know without talking?"

"Yahh?" Sofia nods, black curls bouncing affirmatively.

"Well, she is speaking to me now."

I look up and meet Sofia's dark eyes to make sure she believes me. She flutters her upturned lashes, eyes wide and waiting. Her eyes are totally trusting and interested. There is no sign of doubt in them.

"She says that um, tonight is the Aquarius New Moon and a good night for beginnings." I shake my head. "I swear Sof, like I am such a realist this is alot for me to take in but it's real and she is here ...now."

The air between us shimmers like a ripple of water. I don't see it because I am looking at Sofia but she does.

"I believe you," she says pointing to the ripple and turning off the lantern.

Glimmering bands of violet, emerald, and silver light moving like electrical currents begin to outline my Grandmother's form.

Sofia and I sit perfectly still, watching. Starlight illuminates the dancing colored lines of Gram's spirit or essence or whatever you want to call it and the night is suddenly very quiet and still. "Girls," sings Gram in her beautiful birdlike voice, "I am pleased to be with you tonight."

I reach out for her but feel nothing. My hand passes through electric looking color bands like the dark moon on a solar eclipse. She continues.

"For certain people, vortexes are indeed entryways to other dimensions, even galaxies. Certain people like you, Lena and Sofia..."

Silence.

Through the moon roof, the planet Venus shines her light on us and a shooting star flames across the sky.

"Can you hear her, Sof?" I ask. "It sounds like she is talking to both of us this time."

I put my hand on Sofia's arm hoping with all my heart she hears Gram and it isn't just me.

"I hear her, girl," Sofia whispers.

I feel the goose bumps on her skin. She wraps her arm around my shoulders and I wrap mine around her waist. Our heads tilt together and we sit watching Gram's shimmering spirit move like an extraordinary light show for us only. Different parts of her illuminate for a second at a time before changing like Christmas lights shining on her eyes, arms, mouth, hair, hands, and so on. It's pretty and calming. It has us in a trance.

"Lena and Sofia," Gram continues, "you come from a long line of powerful women with special gifts. Astral travel, teleportation, telepathy, and communication with elementals and intergalactic beings among them. Once in a while the gifts skip a generation to simmer and stew for greater strength in the following generation...as in your cases. As you well know, neither of your mothers has them."

Sofia and I look at each other, memories of childhood and wondering why we felt so different from other kids pour through our minds in a sort of mental share.

"Because the gifts skipped your mothers, I suspect they will be strong in the both of you. They are your birthright to use and craft as you please. The only requirement is," a long pause, "you must promise to use your gifts for the good of all beings and not just for selfish gains."

Silence.

"Do you girls, Lena and Sofia, promise to use your gifts for the good of all beings and not for selfish gains? I need to hear you speak the words aloud. When you speak the words and mean them in your hearts, your gifts will be made available. The elements and ...most intergalactic beings are your friends, girls, so do not be afraid."

I am the first to speak, "Should we think about it awhile first? It seems like a pretty big commitment."

Sofia elbows me in the ribs. I jump and sputter in surprise. "Speak for yourself girlfriend. I am ready for my gifts. Can't you feel that ...this is how it's supposed to be?"

I sit for a minute and breathe in the dark with Gram's shimmering spirit and Sofia's gorgeous wild haired dark outline, the starry sky above us swirling with ancestral yesterdays and infinite tomorrows. The blood in my veins and the marrow in my bones reach for the promise and the gifts that I know are mine. I will not overthink this because I *feel it*.

"I promise to use my gifts for the good of all beings and not just for selfish gains," I whisper meaning every word more than I've ever meant anything in my life.

"I promise to use my gifts for the good of all beings and not just for selfish gains," Sofia says confidently squeezing my shoulder.

"Very good girls. You've welcomed the elements in your own unique way and you've taken the vow of One Universe. Because you are old souls with lifetimes of passing tests and learning skills behind you, there are no more requirements. Congratulations. Your ancestral gifts are now available." Grams voice issuing from her shimmering color shape sounds like it's passing through a waterfall, wind and a flute before reaching us.

As I try to remember her living voice to make the comparison, she holds her left hand up to the sky palm facing out and extends her right hand towards us palm face up. From the center of her right electric spirit palm a purple swirl, a white grey feather, a gold flame, a blue drop of water, and a green leaf emerge one after another quickly and then duplicate.

One line of elemental symbols enters Sofia's left ear and one line enters my right ear.

ZAP ZAP ZING!

If I blinked I would have missed it. That fast.

I turn to look at Sofia.

Her eyes are all zen and calm. *"Did you see that?"* I think at her. *"Yes,"* she thinks back.

"Did you feel anything?" "No."

"Me neither."

"Listen," Gram says, "to know the sounds the elements will use to alert you when they require your attention."

So we listen to the elements inside of us and I hear, as if am wearing the world's best headphones.

Static as Space, the purple swirl. Wind as Air, the white grey feather. Crackling as Fire, the gold flame. Waterfall as Water, the blue drop. Deep, low rumbling as Earth, the green leaf.

And then everything gets super quiet again. We sit for a long time just breathing.

When I feel like Gram is about to leave, I ask, "Who wrote this book, *Sleeping Lady Mountain Magic: Elemental Vortexes* and why was it left for Sofia?"

I take the book off Sofia's lap and hold it up to Gram's lightshow.

She answers farther away, like she is speaking from a greater distance this time, "Sofia's great, great grandmother on her mother's side wrote this book. It has held up remarkably well."

"*My* great-great-grandmother on my mother's side!? My Cherokee great-great-grandma?" Sofia asks incredulously and so loud a dog starts barking in the neighbor's yard. "But my Mom was adopted and I didn't even know my blood grandma. So how did it end up in our new house on a bookshelf in *my room*?"

"Never underestimate the powers that be, dear one. Our family lines have a long history of women working with elementals and intergalactic beings for the greater good. A little thing like adoption would never stop ancestral knowledge and soul evolution in the bloodline."

Gram chuckles like a running stream and wind chimes.

"You mean Sofia's family and ours, Gram? Our families have known each other a long time?" I ask making sure I understand.

"Yes, Lena Lenora. Your friendship with Sofia was written in the stars long ago just like Sofia's grandmother and I were friends and their mothers before that..."

"You and Sofia's grandmom were friends?" I interrupt dumb-founded, "But how?"

"Learn to accept what is without having to know every detail dear. I will tell you one day... As I was saying, you two will always be able to communicate with each other telepathically no matter where you are near or far. Isn't that fun?" Gram's laugh tinkles like a bell in the night.

The neighbor's dog stops barking.

"Yeah and way better than cell phones," Sofia laughs too. "Super old school amazing," she says taking the book from my hands and holding it to her heart. "So what kind of gifts do we have, uh Lena's Grandma? I don't know much about my Mom's family so all of this is new to me," a sheepish smile spreads across her face and I can see her blushing in the dark.

"You may call me Rose, dear one, as that was my name on Earth this past life. As far as gifts go, you will be able to communicate with Earth's messengers, elementals of Earth, Fire, Water, Air, and Ether. You may even be able to travel into their realms. You may have the opportunity to sit in or join the Galactic Council like your great-great-grandmothers before you. I do not know how everything will unfold as free will is always at play. You will have to discover for yourselves."

Gram's shimmering spirit begins to fade from the bottom up. Her light lines break into a million pixels and dissipate in front of our eyes.

Violet, blue, green, and white tiny stars dissolve into the black night.

She is gone as fast as she appeared.

Just like that in and out of a ripple in the air.

"I hope my gifts are better than yours," Sofia's eyes light up with humor and excitement.

When I don't laugh, she taps my leg like you know I am kidding right and I do but my brain is working overtime right now to digest all of this.

Maybe I should have thought about it a day before promising to use my gifts only for good. Because being the face of Wüter is pretty selfish. I'm doing it for money, to start my acting career, and to make my dad and uncle happy. Doesn't that make me just as bad as them? Or is making enough money to start a water cleanup campaign when I turn 18 or whatever a good enough reason to do it?

I am tired.

The need for sleep overtakes me. I lay down in the soft nest of sleeping bags and pillows. It is almost one am. I close my eyes.

TWENTY

The sound of lawn mowers in the morning wakes me. It is so stifling hot in the tent it must be past nine. I reach for my warm lavender lemonade, shake it, take a sip.

I promise to use my gifts for the good of all beings and not just for selfish gains.

These words roll through my mind like a mantra.

Sofia is still asleep; beads of sweat on her forehead, dark curls damp. *Sleeping Lady Mountain Magic: Elemental Vortexes* peeks out from under her pillow.

I unzip the front entrance quietly, crawl out, and head inside for a cool, one-minute shower.

I promise to use my gifts for the good of all beings and not just for selfish gains.

In the shower, I wash and condition my hair quickly. I towel off and apply shea butter moisturizer before pulling on jean shorts and a tee shirt. Then toss a pillow in the middle of the rug for a much-needed mini meditation.

Gram immediately joins me.

"Honey, I am so proud of you for accepting your gifts and the responsibilities that go with them! Today you will have the chance to test your abilities at the local Earth Vortex. It's a perfect first-time meeting ground and the Earth elementals and inter-galactics are excited to meet you. Use the map in the book, begin the lesson, and I'll meet you there. Oh, and make sure to explain to Sofia about meditation. She needs to do it too to maintain her powers and stay energetically clear."

I don't respond to Gram this time but will do as she asks. Sitting cross legged on the pillow, I close my eyes and watch my thoughts.

What if I change my mind about the gifts in a few weeks or a few years? What if I just want to be normal at some point? Can I give them back or tell them to go away?

An iced mocha would be nice right now. Maybe we can get one on the way to the vortex.

Will we ever go back to Wilmington or will we stay here? Will we ever be able to swim or drink the water there again?

Am I doing the right thing being in the Wüter commercial?

So many questions! Ahhhh. Shut off mind!

Gram knows I am worrying and says soothingly, *"Honey, don't worry about all that right now, one day at a time. You will be fine. Just enjoy this time of expansion and learning! I am here to support you every step of the way and so is Sofia. I'll see you at*

*the Earth Vortex! Whoo hoo! My grand-daughter has her gifts;
our lineage is not dead!"*

Excited and confused, I have no idea what to expect. I don't even
think I can tell Kiki Astromatrix this one. I might have to keep it
a secret. Feeling like I am in another world already, I remember
the *Star Seed Nation Alert* I heard the day before the hurricane. I
wonder if I can find it again?

I flip open my laptop and search 'Star Seed Nation Alert June
2025.' Nothing comes up. Was it erased?

Trying the exact date yields better results, 'June 7, 2025 Star
Seed Nation Alert.' Ok here it is. I click and listen.

"Earth is ascending. The purification process, what humans call
'extreme weather,' is preparing the planet and its inhabitants for
her new position in the fifth dimension.

To increase the chances of human survival during this process,
The Galactic Council is stepping in, actively recruiting high
vibration young people known throughout the galaxy as "New
Earth Star Seeds" to join mission NEAR, *New Earth Advanced
Recalibration.*

The mission itself while simple in nature requires a large team of
high frequency youth to Implement. New Earth Star Seeds will
naturally be drawn to the recruitment. If you are listening to this
message, chances are you are a Star Seed.

Other signs you are a Star Seed include extreme sensitivity to
and refusal to absorb violence in any form including
entertainment and news. Extreme sensitivity to chemicals,
pharmaceuticals, alcohol and drugs, questioning authority
when something

doesn't seem right, a feeling that you are a part of something greater than daily life, a feeling that you have not always lived on Earth, being a big picture thinker, caring immensely about the planet and all of life, possessing a sixth sense, having an ancestor with a sixth sense, and or having an ancestor who has been in contact with Extraterrestrials are all signs that you are a New Earth Star Seed.

If you are a person born in the 21st century with three or more of these qualifications, the Galactic Council is looking for you! Two seats urgently need filled in the United States chapter of the GC. Two seats... ask yourself, could one be yours? Star Seed youth, step to the calling now."

"New Earth Star Seed," I say aloud. "Mission NEAR."

Over three million people have watched this video.

1,350,579 'liked' it.

I stare at the screen. Then get up and walk to my vanity. "I cannot stand violence," I say looking at my reflection. "My friends call me Lena PG and make it sound like a bad thing."

I put peppermint oil on my wrists then put a few drops on my ankles to deter ticks. A few minutes later, a knock on my bedroom door.

"How did you sleep, hon?" Mom pokes her head in my room as I'm pulling on hiking shoes.

If she only knew! "Good," I shrug sitting just outside my closet.

"Did you guys have fun?"

"Mm-hm."

"What are you doing today?"

"Going for a hike with Sofia and her dog." I say rummaging in the closet for my daypack. "He's used to running free on land and feels cooped up. Think you can drop us off at the trail head by the lake after breakfast?"

"You mean you two and the *dog*?" Mom wrinkles her nose.

I know it's because she doesn't want dog hair in her new car.

"Smokey is a clean dog, Mom. He has short hair and we can put a beach towel down." I suddenly feel very impatient with Mom's clean freak, worry wart, workaholic ways.

Mom continues to make the face.

"Fine, don't worry about it then. We'll ask Sofia's aunt. She won't mind." I say curtly with a wave of my hand, throwing my daypack over my shoulder.

"Ask her aunt this time hon, I'm at a good point in my book and don't want to stop and get off track." Mom's tone is warm and apologetic yet I remain annoyed.

She tries to hug me but I walk past her fluffing my wet hair on the way out. I feel mean but do it anyway.

"Don't forget your sunscreen!" Mom calls after me, "And be home for dinner!"

"Your book better make the best seller list..." I grumble under my breath running down the stairs.

"Hey," Sofia says wiping sleep out of her eyes at the bottom of the steps. "I need a shower. Which bathroom should I use?"

"Use mine. Go up the stairs to the right all the way down the hall, it's in the room with all of the boxes. I have a towel ready for you."

"Thanks," Sofia says heading upstairs. "Meet me in the kitchen after!"

Sofia showers quickly and we convene in the kitchen eating cereal together and making what sense we can of the Earth Vortex chapter and map in *Sleeping Lady Mountain Magic: Elemental Vortexes.*

"Ok, so it looks like the Earth Vortex is a few miles up past those caves where my Dad took us to mine for emeralds," I say comparing her great-great-grandmother's hand drawn illustration in the book to a Gogle map of Black Mountain hiking trails. I am very good at reading maps; it is something Dad taught me.

"How can you tell?" Sofia asks scrunching her nose. "I can't make heads or tails of this thing."

"I just know," I say. "I've been coming here every summer since I was born. Gram was a hiker and Dad used to love to pan for gold and mine for gems. We've been all over these mountains."

"Your dad's a gold miner?"

"Ha!" I laugh imagining Dad in overalls and dirt on his face panning for gold for work. "No, he's a lawyer and investor but we used to do that for fun. Like when we were little, he took us..."

I zoom in on the trailhead, mapping the distance from Daffodil House to the drop off point. It is 12.1 miles.

"Wow," Sofia breathes impressed, "Did you ever find gold or emeralds?"

"Yep," I nod. "Remind me to show you my raw emerald collection later. They're different than emeralds in jewelry stores because they haven't been cut or polished but they're pretty."

I fill two flasks with tap water, the bottle of Wüter just because, two apples, and two sandwiches in the main compartment of my backpack, and stash my cell phone, for the map, in a separate compartment.

"It's crazy your great-great grandma wrote that book, huh?" I say watching Sofia lovingly trace the word Earth with her fingers.

"It's crazy *your Grandma* appears out of thin air!" Sofia says curtly.

Our eyes meet and we laugh because what else can we do? We are in this together, friends for life. However short or long that is.

"Dude, did she say both of our great-great grandmothers were on the Galactic Council?"

"I think she did. It's kind of a blur right now, honestly," I say massaging Sofia's shoulders while looking over them at the map. "Can you read the Earth vortex communication thingy one more time before we go, please?"

"That feels good, go harder on my right shoulder... and sure," she says opening to the lesson. "Earth. Earth is a living being who loves and supports all of life. To establish a clear communication with Earth elementals go to the Earth Vortex and create a circle of stone. Sing while you work. Take off your shoes before entering the circle. Sit in the circle. Press your right hand to Earth and your left hand to your heart. Recite the following:

"Beloved Mother Earth. We, your children, love and respect you! Your ancient magic is in our bones. We call to you to establish a healing communication. Send for us when you will. We have come."

"Okay, cool," I exhale loudly with horse lips. "Is your aunt on her way with Smokey?"

"Yeah," Sofia stands up, "Should we bring the book with us?"

"I'd like to but its up to you. I wouldn't wanna ruin it." "Let's bring it. I want it too."

"We can put it in a ziplock bag…" "Good idea."

Beep! Beep! Aunt Laurie is out front. I grab a large plastic Zip Lock freezer bag from the pantry to protect the book, and we dash out the door.

TWENTY-ONE

Aunt Laurie is waiting for us in an old Grey Volkswagen convertible, top down, windows up, listening to country music. Smokey is standing on the back seat looking very excited to see us.

The North Carolina sky is a calm, clear blue like nothing could be wrong in the world. A hummingbird stops directly in front of my face as I walk down the sidewalk towards the VW convertible. The colorful little bird hovers and sprints left and right, then left and right again at eye level.

"I love you too, friend," I say under my breath watching it fly away.

"That was weird," says Sofia. "That hummingbird was like right in your face like looking at you."

"That happens a lot. They like me for some reason maybe because I use essential oil, they think I am a flower," I laugh.

Bark one. Bark two. Smokey's excited 'I am happy to see you bark' slices through thick summer air with a high pitch whiny ring.

I open the back door and climb in. "Hi, boy!"

Sofia gets in front, "Thank you, Aunt Laurie!" she kisses her aunt on the cheek.

Aunt Laurie says, "No problem, Kiddo. Aunt Laurie's Taxi at your service."

"Ha Ha! You're kiddo too." I laugh. "My Dad calls me that like *all the time*." I roll my eyes and giggle.

"What? No more kiddo?" Aunt Laurie asks Sofia. "No, it's fine. I don't mind."

"Good, 'caus you'll always be kiddo to me. Where to?" Aunt Laurie asks Sofia who turns to me for directions.

"Ask the tour guide here. Lena is like a genius with maps." "Okay," I say all animated with hand gestures, feeling very grown up and responsible. "There is a dog friendly trail about twelve miles from here. Take Main Street towards the lake and make a left right before you see the park entrance sign. The trail head is a mile from there."

I pat Smokey's broad chest. Weimaraner's have huge rib cages and slim waists. When I pat his chest it sounds like a drum.

"You got it, girls! Buckle up!" Aunt Laurie winks at me in the rear view, lights a cigarette, and takes off ...fast. Smokey falls face first into the middle console and I let out a girlish squeal that pretty much throws my feeling grown up right out the window.

Smokey rights himself.

I hold onto him and he leans into me. Aunt Laurie chuckles.

Being from Montana, Aunt Laurie hasn't adjusted to the slower speed limits in the south yet... trees fly past. Another driver yells at us.

Would it be rude for me to ask her to slow down?

I wish Mom wasn't so attached to her book sometimes and would at least pick us up later. I make a mental note to not ask Aunt Laurie to drive us anywhere again.

The Montana plated convertible jerks to a halt. I roll my window down and jump out quickly, not bothering to open the door. Smokey follows me; nose to the ground immediately. Sofia, apparently used to high speed driving, lingers to give her aunt a hug and ask her to pick us up at 5pm, six hours from now.

"Sure you girls wanna be out that long," Aunt Laurie wrinkles her forehead and scrunches her nose. "It's hot ...and humid. Y'all will be puddles of sweat come five."

We nod in unison.

"Ok, suit yourselves. Y'all have your cell-phones right?" "Yes, Aunty, we do." Sofia says. "See you at five and thanks!"

We smile and wave to Aunt Laurie as the grey Volkswagen disappears down the road in a cloud of dust, country music, and cigarette smoke.

"Has your aunt ever been in an accident?" I ask. "Not that I know of," Sofia says.

"Good," I say and leave it at that.

It is a steady uphill hike to the crystal caves where Earth Vortex is. Smokey takes the lead and we make our way up into the mountain. The forest welcomes us with the delicious sharp scent of all things alive and green and a much cooler temperature than our in-town homes.

As the tree line thickens, the forest floor becomes intricately laced with jutting button mushrooms and twirling green ferns. A carpet of soft cushy moss and pine needles adds a refreshing bounce to our step. Wildflowers appear like little welcoming friends.

Orange tiger lily and yellow fawn lily shout exuberant welcomes of hello, hi, and over here! White Iris and delicate pink rose claim beauty enhancement and happy heart benefits. Pink shooting stars point us in the direction of the vortex, shy violets whisper among themselves, and regal wild orchids stand tall and erect bowing slightly as we pass, "They're here, they're here! The bridges are here."

Further along the trail on getting into high altitude, we are greeted by Indian Pipe, a ghostly white flower the shape of a peace pipe with a "How." A little further up, Ginseng the five leaved medicinal plant with bright red berries asks, "Need some extra energy?"

"Do you hear the flowers?" I ask Sofia.

"What do you mean?" she says. "I *see* the flowers but I don't *hear* the flowers."

"Oh, well, I hear them. I guess its part of my power then and not yours."

"They're *talking to you*? What are they saying?" Sofia asks. "What happens if you step on one by accident?"

"Yah, they're talking. They're just saying group stuff like

hello, welcome and telling me what they're used for."

"Oh," says Sofia squinting her eyes and straining to listen. I giggle. "Why are you squinting to listen?"

"Was I squinting?"

"Ya, you looked super funny too." Like this, and I show her. She giggles, "I guess that's my concentration face."

"These pink ones that look like shooting stars keep telling us how to get to the vortex," I say bending down to touch a tiny pink petal. "I think the different families of wildflowers are like a single mind organism, kinda like a school of fish swim as one, ya know? The roses and irises tell me they have beauty benefits and the ...that one over there, Ginseng, says it will give us extra energy if we need it."

"What would they say if we step on one of them? Ouch?

Would it hurt?"

"I don't know. Probably nothing," I say. "I think it would be like me pulling one hair out of your head. You are the same...not much changes."

"Oh. That makes sense."

Smokey barks up ahead. Ruff one, ruff two, ruff three, his alert bark.

Sofia whistles her low come here whistle and he bounds towards us.

"What do you think he's barking at?" I ask nervously.

"He probably heard something. He's a good watchdog, not a protector like a German Shepherd. Once when I was hiking with friends in Montana there was a guy with a gun shooting target practice. Smokey hid behind me."

I laugh imagining that. "Oh my gosh! Was everything ok though?"

"Ya. Turned out to be one of my friend's dads. I am just saying Smokey is not a guard dog only a watchdog. So ya know. If anything did happen we'd be on our own with our...gifts."

"Hey, we're not supposed to think afraid thoughts," I say. "Why?"

"Because of the Law of Attraction, what you think about you attract. So only think good thoughts, okay?"

"Totally. I am not scared anyway, are you?"

"No."

We continue hiking up the mountain in silence, me listening to the flowers and Sofia looking and listening for her own gifts.

TWENTY-TWO

Quarter mile from the caves, the temperature drops like 10 degrees. The low rumbling earth element alert sounds in our inner ears followed by a message that we should take off our shoes. We do so immediately, depositing them under a huge tree to retrieve on the way back down.

Earth is humming here.

I feel it under my bare feet vibrating and alive. We are getting close to the vortex.

The power is calm and strong and peaceful.

I feel the way I did whenever Mom, Gram, and I were together like there is more of me than me. Like being who I am makes sense. Evolving from a great long line of powerful women not just from Mom and Dad. I am capable of anything, and we're all connected to Earth and to the Universe.

Sofia sends me a mental confirmation that she feels the same, powerful, strong, like our ancestors are with us. Our entire maternal lineage, grandmothers, great-grandmothers, and great-great grandmothers, infinity.

We hold hands and walk up the mountain barefoot. Walking slower now and more deliberate, connecting with Earth every step we take. Our feet feel every twig and patch of moss we touch. Earth power, cool and strong and green, fills us; our feet, our legs, hips, bellies, arms, necks and heads. The power feels almost heavy when it reaches the top of my head. It is not electric but vibrates and thrums cool, strong, nourishing and deep.

Gradually the steep incline levels out to a flat clearing with tall trees bordering the outskirts like guards. In the middle of the clearing are the crystal caves. Dark stacking limestone caverns with a wide gaping mouth covered in green black moss. Clear clumps of hanging crystals catch rays of light at the mouth of the cave, which is sort of triangular.

Beyond it and to the right is a fast-moving stream noisily alive with several small rushing waterfalls in a row cascading over smooth, colorful rock slick with moss. The humming vibration of Earth is a rumbling lullaby up here, deep, low, and soothing with a slight taste of metal and dirt.

Suddenly very hungry and thirsty, I pull my backpack off and take out the hydro-flasks and sandwiches. Sofia and I sit by the stream and eat and drink. We have been hiking steady uphill over two hours. The sandwiches taste good and the tap water is the best tasting water I ever had.

"I am grateful for this water," I say and mean it. "Do you know what my Dad does for a living?"

"You told me but I forget. What?"

"Defends bad guys," I say bluntly reaching for my apple. "He's a big business lawyer. His biggest ongoing case is defending a monster company that's been dumping a crazy cancerous chemical in the Cape Fear River, the water source in Wilmington… where I'm from, since before I was born. So full of chemicals you can't drink it without major purification and now…you can't drink it all. People used to picket on our lawn." I hang my head.

"That's not your fault, girl. You are not your father." Sofia puts a reassuring hand on my back and rubs little circles between my shoulders.

"There's more." I pick up a pebble and roll it between my fingers. I throw it into the stream and watch it disappear in the white gurgle of clean mountain water.

Water is life. You are water. Water is life. I hear it say.

"Ok? What?"

"So, my Dad and his brother, my Uncle Leo, he makes commercials in Hollywood…they invest in the same companies together sometimes… to make money. Like they invest in oil, silver, chemicals, AI, and now…they're investing in a water substitute called Wüter."

I find a base rock and begin building a rock pile altar. I place a smaller rock on top of the base then place a third and fourth rock. The fifth rock makes the pile tumble and I begin again.

"They want me to be the face of it or something, like do a commercial. I mean I'm a pretty good actress and I wanna do commercials and movies one day but ...not this kind, not for something bad." I wipe a tear from my cheek, pick up another pebble, roll it between my fingers, and toss it. "A water substitute is like really scary. Don't you think?"

"Hell ya, girl! That is scary! Have you tasted it?"

"I had a sip. I brought it in case you wanted to try it."

I pull the Wüter out and hand it over to Sofia.

"Woowww and your face could be on this next year huh?" I grimace.

"I mean, they said this thing is gonna take off and I could make a lot of money. They'll probably sit on it 'til I'm 18 but that's only three years. Then I could buy you a bike no problem, and a cool car. We could go anywhere we want."

"Money is something." Sofia shakes the Wüter, opens it and sniffs it like they do in wine tasting. "But not everything. I mean imagine if we couldn't swim in the oceans or rivers or drink clean water ever again! I would die!"

"That's pretty much the point, Sof. We would probably all die or be like super sickly."

She takes a gulp of the Wüter and sticks out her tongue. "It's a little thick... but I guess its ok... I mean I wouldn't wanna drink it all the time, you know? Yuck. Want the rest of it?"

Wrinkling her nose, she passes me the Wüter.

"No thanks." I pour the rest on the ground. It doesn't sink in, just kinda sits there.

"It's not sinking in! See that?"

"Yah. Earth doesn't want it either." I put the empty plastic bottle in my backpack. "Well lunch was good, huh?" I say a bit fake, trying to change the mood. "I am grateful for this moment. Who knows how long people will have beautiful mountains to hike and real water to drink."

"Me too, girl. I am grateful," Sofia slaps me on the back for emphasis a little too hard and makes a crazy face. "Now let's build that stone circle."

Sofia has this knack for being funny and serious at the same time. I think that's called a dry sense of humor. She is so good at it that sometimes I don't know whether to laugh or ...what.

Wiping her mouth with the back of her hand, Sofia tosses a salivating Smokey her last bit of bologna and cheese then rinses her hands in the stream. I toss Smokey the bite I saved for him too. Our guide dog deserves a snack!

I rinse my hands, face and neck in the cold, clear stream and twist my damp hair up in a bun on the very top of my head.

Then, while Smokey splashes all the way into the stream drinking his fill and cooling off, Sofia and I set to work finding medium, hand sized rocks to make the circle, taking our time to choose the ones that call to us. I am bent over inspecting a rock when I hear Sofia begin to sing.

"The next generation of bridges are here to speak with Mother Earth. The next generation of bridges have come to take our

place in line. We are that generation. Behold our generation. The next generation of bridges have come to speak with Mother Earth!"

I look over at her. She has a silver white glow about her from head to toe; her voice is low and sweet. Everything seems to bend to her as she sings. Trees, flowers, even the stream takes a slightly closer path to her magnetic voice.

"Where did you learn that?" I ask.

"I just made it up right now," Sofia smiles. "What's a bridge?"

"We are, I think. Do you like it?"

"I love it! Mind if I sing with you? Maybe that's one of *your* gifts, weaving songs and actually you're pretty good at story-telling too," I say placing a rock in the circle. "Does singing that song feel like a power? 'Caus it feels pretty powerful to me. Like it's etched in my mind already. I don't even need to ask you to repeat it. I could chime right in!"

"It is a power or a...a gift," Sofia says. "It feels buzzy on my insides and in my head. Do I look different? I feel kind of magnetic in the soles of my feet and hands. Like I am pulling things to me."

"You are glowing," I tell her. "You have a silvery-whitish glow. The flowers and grass... everything was like *bending towards you* when you were singing. So maybe you are magnetic."

"The book says sing while we build the circle, right? And my great-great grandma wrote it so...maybe I've done it before. It all feels pretty natural."

So we sing together. We sing the song and build the circle, slow, steady, and deliberate.

"The next generation of bridges is here to speak with Mother Earth. The next generation of bridges has come to take our place in line. We are that generation. Behold our generation. The next generation of bridges has come to speak with Mother Earth!"

It takes a half an hour to complete the circle. We make it nice and even all the way around. At 2:22pm we enter the circle barefoot and kneel down facing each other. Hearts full of song, sweaty, tired but excited, with no idea what to expect.

Smokey does not come near the circle. Instead, he chooses a comfy spot in the shade of a tree in viewing distance, and drifts off to sleep, gray face between his paws.

The rumbling of Earth is a constant low buzzing sound. The glow from the crystal cave, which grew in strength and brightness, as the circle grew, is by now like a stage light shining out.

Sofia has a silver aura.

"Did you ever see one of those Renaissance paintings with the gold halos behind people's heads," she asks me.

"Yeah?"

"That's what you look like but it's all around you not just your head."

"Really?" I lift my hands to my face to look but can't see my own glow. I see Sofia's though. "Dude, *you* are totally outlined in silver light!"

"Did you just call me dude in a sacred circle?" Sofia laughs. "I feel like we should be wearing ceremonial garb or something not sweaty street clothes." She lifts her arm to look for the silver glow and shrugs.

"Should we take a picture?"

A definitive 'no' comes to mind. "No blue light here it will weaken the vortex."

"I got that message too," Sofia frowns. "Loud and clear like.

Do you know who said it?"

"No freakin' clue. Maybe our higher self or spirit guide? I know she's good and I can trust her. I do know that."

"Okay. Me too. No pictures then. Ready?" "Yes, you?"

"Yes."

Placing our right hand to Earth and left hand to our hearts, we say together the words from the book:

"Beloved Mother Earth. We, your children, love and respect you! Your ancient magic is in our bones. We call to you to establish a healing communication. Send for us when you will. We have come."

Immediately shiny bits of mica dust particles float up off of

the ground, hover, and speed towards us like shooting stars crowding in on us. In the blink of an eye, those dust particles turn into pixelated light beings and we are not alone. Within minutes the partially see through pixelated beings evolve into human holograms and other worldly forms and walk towards the circle of stone.

Our ancestors, I hope? Yes, I can feel it.

Native American, African American, dark eyed Italian women plus tall slim female shapes from other planets I suppose materialize on Sofia's side, and fall into place behind her in the West.

Fair skin, light haired Irish, English, and Scottish women plus tall slim beings from other planets materialize and move towards me, filling the space around me in the East.

Every powerful woman in our maternal lineage is here right now. There are thousands of us. Scanning the sea of faces for Gram, I find her directly behind me.

She smiles. Earth continues to hum. Visions appear within the circle of stones. Ancestral memories pour forth into the air.

Women sitting in circles in animal skins. Women sitting in circles in long dresses. Women walking together hand in hand. Women giving birth. Women with dogs. Women with children. Women in the mountains. Women with wolves and bears and coyotes and hawks and raccoons. Women from other worlds with glowing orbs moving about their heads. Women working together.

Like flashes on a movie screen, the visions keep coming. At one point I look up and the entire forest floor is jam packed with women, spirits, and other worldly beings with large, dark eyes like deer.

Sofia is directly across from me.

I think at her, *"Can you believe this? How are you doing?"* *"I feel strong, girl. These are our ancestors. How are you?"*

"I feel strong, too. What the heck is going to happen do you think?" "I have no idea!"

Buzzing. Humming. Vibrating.

High frequency sound emitting from the crystal cave pours forth over the clearing. The hazy light turns blue green then clear again. From the depths of the cave, a figure emerges still in shadow. The sound gets so high pitched we can no longer hear it.

The green face of a woman appears. Her eyes are large and dark like an elephants with long lashes. Within them I see the universe dark and deep and infinite. Two arms materialize next, her torso, one leg then the other until a strong, medium framed, sturdy green woman with leaves in her hair, gold dust on her forehead, and long wavy auburn hair materializes fully.

In an instant, she moves from the mouth of the cave to the center of the circle. No, she doesn't move, she transfers. One second she's at the cave, the next in the circle.

The buzzing in the forest grows to a crescendo until we can no longer hear the noisy stream. Then silence. Waiting.

All faces turn towards the green woman.

She is wearing a dress made of brown and gold leaves. Her feet and hands are square, small, and earth like. Thick wavy auburn hair the color of fall maple leaves, is tucked behind two large flat ears and matches her eyebrows perfectly.

Henna, I think.

But this is an elemental!

This is not a woman who shops at Ulta.

"Girls, says Green Lady all low and rumbly and sweet. "Young women," she says tipping her head and smiling baring strong yellow white teeth at us. "As Head Earth Elemental, I am most pleased to welcome you to this humble yet powerful Earth Vortex. We have not had the pleasure of meeting traveling bridge communicators at this location for a hundred years so this is a very special occasion indeed," she beams.

Murmurs and nods of approval float among the sea of spirited ancestral faces.

Clicks and whirs, tinkles, and tings fill the clearing. I shiver.

"Bring the gifts!" Green Lady claps."

From within the crowd, two large leaves are passed around and move towards us, stopping in front of us. The leaves hover in front of us, our gifts wrapped inside.

We hold out our hands and the leaves descend gently into our upturned palms. I open my leaf and gasp.

In it, a most beautiful half thumb sized glowing white crystal on a delicate gold necklace for me; silver for Sofia.

I blink. My logical mind rears up. I try hard to think of something to say but can't find any words. Can any of this be real? Oh, but we are way past that now!

"There is an entire world *inside* of Earth girls and you two have an invitation to visit, even be a part of it if you choose. Your crystal quartz pendants, pure hearts, and the ancestral magic in your bones," the green lady winks and there is laughing and nodding among the crowd, "is your key into our realm."

When you want to be transported to Inner Earth, think of the stone circle you created, think of your lineage, and hold your crystal between your thumb and first finger. If you are indeed traveling bridge communicators, as we believe you are, you will be instantly transported."

Sofia is already wearing her crystal pendant. I put mine on too with shaky hands missing the clasp several times before I get it right. It fits perfectly once I do get it and feels like a protective bliss bubble just burst around me like a coat of shining armor. A gift from an elemental, from Inner Earth!

"Thank you, Green Lady! I love it" Sofia says.

A low rumbling earthquake of a laugh from Green Lady shakes the entire forest floor. "Love, yes. Good. Please... call me Arghata."

"Thank you, Arghata," we say again in unison.

She nods smiling broadly. Chest held high, perfect posture and a sturdy stance.

"I love mine too, Arghata!" I exclaim, one hand over my heart. "It feels ...protective."

"You are most welcome and you are also correct. This is a very protective gift indeed. For when you wear it, you will never have to worry about perishing in a hurricane, flood, tornado, wildfire or any kind of extreme weather set forth by Earth messengers. You are one of us in a sense and we need you. We need... each other," Arghata nods spreading upturned hands in a semi-circle in front of her chest.

Noises of approval and acknowledgment float among the spirit crowd.

Arghata continues, "I would like you to test your ability by traveling once to Inner Earth and back again. We have time. There is a round table.... how do you say...meeting you should attend. It is happening now."

Looking us up and down, a slow smile spreads across her face as she places her hand on her heart, "I believe you *will* attend. Now, think of the stone circle you created, sing your song internally, hold on to your crystals and if you are indeed *traveling* bridge communicators as we believe you to be, you will be transported to outer Inner Earth immediately."

Arghata gestures to us like an orchestra conductor to hold on to our pendants.

We hold on with our pointer finger and thumb, think of the circle, and close our eyes. Warm and cool air surround us followed by a generator sound and finally, thick silence. For a split second, I am moving through a sort of goo and falling through space.

TWENTY-THREE

When we open our eyes we are standing on slate grey floors surrounded by white crystal walls with the slightest tint of pink. There is no jolt or miss-step from either of us. It's like we are just here like the next scene of a movie.

Emeralds, amethysts, and clear and grey crystal quartz jut randomly from the ceiling and through the floor. The lighting is hazy like dawn or dusk. It is pleasantly cool but a little hard to breathe.

"Are we inside of Earth right now?" I ask.

"I think so," says Sofia running her finger over a large, jagged amethyst shaped like an iceberg.

We walk for a few minutes down gently sloping hallways, our footsteps not making a sound. I stop to touch a large raw emerald after nearly tripping over it. An upside-down triangle shaped door appears on the left. We approach and it slides up.

Arghata is seated at a huge gray slab desk in a highly advanced office wearing a dark blue-black shimmering pants suit with gold neckband and cuffs, looking comfortably presidential. Her auburn hair is braided in one long braid which hangs over her shoulder, banded in gold at the bottom. Gold Egyptian looking pyramid earrings jut from her small ears. There is an office in Inner Earth?!

I think of my Mom slaving over her book and David in VR world in his room.

Be present for this, Lena, I remind myself. Be totally present. I swallow the lump forming in my throat. I am courageous. I am strong. I am love. I am in Inner Earth.

Sofia and I enter the office staring. I grab her hand and squeeze it. She squeezes back. Behind the desk, which looks like it weighs about a thousand pounds, Arghata is perched on a hovering triangle shaped seat, not unlike a bike seat with clear webbing for a back like a lacrosse stick. It changes light patterns on the floor, purple dots, blue fuzz, white, red swirl, purple dots, blue, fuzz white, red swirl.

One wall contains shelves full of rocks and gems all sizes, shapes, and color. The other three walls contain complex maps of the world marked with blinking white, red, and purple lights.

"Welcome to Outer Inner Earth, girls. As I suspected, you *are* able to travel between dimensions."

Arghata touches her throat lightly and hums, "Huuummm- mm." Her throat center lights up with a swirling blue ball of energy.

"I know that mantra," I exclaim bouncing on my bare toes. "It's the throat chakra mantra for communication!   I learned it at yoga!"

"Yoga? Yes. Exercise pants and tank tops. I see it in your mind."

She knits her eyebrows together the blue light at her throat continuing to swirl. "Humans have different words for things. Throat chakra mantra? Yes. It is the sound one evokes before sending a universal communication of importance out."

Arghata stands to make a few notes with her finger on a huge touchscreen and two small white lights on the world map pop up blinking in the southeast corner of the United States.

"You girls are the newest blinking white light. The white lights on this map denote the locations of every Bridge Communicator on Earth."

"Excuse me," I raise my hand like I am in school asking a question.

"Yes," says Arghata nodding in my direction.

"Ahhh, what exactly *are* Bridge Communicators?"

"*You* are a Bridge Communicator, my dear. You and Sofia, like your grandmothers and great grandmothers before you, advanced souls born gifted with telepathy and ... the ability to communicate with all beings *including* elementals and intergalactic races."

"Ah," I raise my hand again.

Arghata raises an eyebrow, one corner of her mouth twitching like she is suppressing laughter. She nods.

"Are all Bridge Communicators girls and women?"

"A very good question, young one! About 65% of BCs on *Earth* are female. 35% are male but really it doesn't make a difference. These are only current statistics."

She makes more markings with the swipe of a short green finger and purple lights appear next to the white lights.

"And this purple light signifies that you are *Traveling Bridge* Communicators, TBCs. Which means as the name suggests, that you are able to travel between dimensions and this... this is very special."

She walks back behind her huge desk and sits on the hovering seat, tenting her fingers together in thought. Her black almond shaped eyes like midnight on the darkest night of the year close. Auburn eyebrows, one unilateral line above them, dip like a "V" in the center. Her throat is still a swirling blue light.

"So eventually we, the head elementals and I of planet Earth, may be asking you to travel between dimensions, even galaxies with important messages- *if* you possess the strength and the foresight to do it. The diseased energy on surface Earth affects everyone, even would be BCs and TBCs. And because they are so sensitive for obvious reasons, many choose some form of escape to block the sensitivity and therefore the ability before we get to them. This is why we recruit young." Arghata sighs.

"We are in desperate need of strong, clear messengers, girls. And in order to do this, you need to stay healthy, strong, and clear. You need to do certain things like avoid toxic media, observe a special diet and daily exercise, be in nature, and speak truth. These basic habits will fortify your birth gifts, your bodies, and minds so that you will always be strong enough to travel on assignment. Traveling between dimensions requires a lot of energy and you will likely need a long sleep after each assignment."

Arghata looks Sofia and I up and down assessing our physical fitness levels. She leans back in her chair and folds her hands.

"How do you feel here in Inner Earth?"

"I feel fine," I say. "I mean it's a little hard to breathe but I feel lighter physically and I am not as worried as I was above ground."

"And you, Sofia?"

"I have a tiny headache but otherwise, I feel the same.

Maybe a little more... lovey... if that makes sense."

Arghata bellows another rumbling earthquake laugh. The gemstones rattle behind her. She puts her legs up on the desk and crosses her ankles. She is wearing soft black slipper booties with gold tipped pyramid laces.

Keeping her feet on the very edge of her desk so as not to disturb the surface items she booms, "As you should feel lovey! There is more love energy in fifth dimension and no hate or violence down here, ugh! As for the headache and feeling hard to breathe that indicates you need more exercise, more water, and more fruit. Simple changes to enhance your comfort in 5D. Now, this is only Outer Inner Earth, girls so really you haven't seen anything yet. Oh but you will! Rule number one of Earth Element: There is absolutely no rushing. No rushing. When you are in Inner Earth you must do things slow, deliberate, precise."

"No rushing," is all I can think to say. "Slow, deliberate, precise," Sofia repeats.

I touch my crystal pendant and look over at Sofia who is calm and relaxed as can be with a doofy smile on her face. I wonder what I look like right now.

"Any more questions?"

"Yes, please," I raise my hand again. "What kind of diet and exercise do we need besides more fruit and water?"

"I will send requirements by messenger within twenty-four hours. Anything else?"

We shake our heads in unison.

"Very good! And although I mentioned no rushing, there is no time to waste either. Galactic Roundtable is taking place at this moment and we want you there. There are things you should know... today. Earth...and all of humanity needs you. Are you ready?"

"Ummm?" I hesitate part of me wishing I was naturally more adventurous and part of me wishing I was home in my comfort zone watching Kiki Astromatrix talk about change rather than actually living the change. This has already been a great adventure so why push it?

While I am hemming and hawing, I hear Sofia say, "Yes!" "Woman!" I exhale through horse lips trying to stay calm.

"Haven't you had enough adventure for one day?"

"Oh, but we've got to be brave, sister! I mean we *are* brave!" she smiles fluttering her curly lashes at me. The light in her dark eyes flashes strength, courage, curiosity, and a long line of powerful ancestry.

As she turns, the crystal quartz pendant swings and shimmers against her navy blue tank top and brown skin, giving Sofia a regal look like a young queen.

"Lena, would you like to attend the meeting or do you prefer to stay in the office and wait? This has to be your decision."

"What? And let her go by herself? No way. I am going too," I announce taking a step closer to Sofia. I stand arrow straight, stretching to my fullest height and puff my chest like a little bird trying to look big.

"Good. Bravery is a quality you must possess and it is well within your reach or you wouldn't be here. Expect to meet beings representing all intergalactic races except the raptor race, elementals, and humans of all ages from all parts of the globe in attendance at Council," she says handing Sofia a silver flask and me one that looks gold. "Glacier water to quench your thirst during the meeting."

Glacier water? Does she know about Wüter I wonder?

Could she?

Sofia and I take the flasks.

"Are you happy wearing surface attire or would you prefer something more galactically appropriate?"

"Something galactically appropriate, please," we croon together anticipating amazing new outfits.

"Good choice," laughs Arghata.

She moves in front of us and closes her eyes. We are instantly clothed in dark blue-black pants suits and booties. Sofia's has a silver neck and wrist cuff detail and my detailing is gold like Arghata's.

The fabric feels like a weightless web, more comfortable than even silk and cotton. There are slim, webby pockets on the sides where normal pockets would be. The booties are a sort of soft leather and very grippy on the bottom.

Amazed at the transformation, I smile like a kid at Christmas. Touching the new fabric, I clap and squeal softly bouncing on my toes.

"Thank you," says Sofia, "Soo much better," spinning around, lifting a leg she points her toe, admiring the booties and pants.

"Now you are ready. Yes?"

"Yes," we nod.

The only wall in the office not covered in crystals and maps opens. We are once again in the crystal corridor. The grey slab floor shines our reflections back at us like a dark mirror.

"Use your intuition and keep your intention pure at Council. Listen more than you speak this time unless asked a direct question and learn," Arghata instructs.

We follow close to her heels like puppies for about 200 feet.

"I will enter here from the back entrance as I normally do. You two walk through the central courtyard and enter from the front. This way you can see some of Inner Earth and I will have a chance to brief council for your arrival."

An orange red triangle door opens. Arghata steps inside and telepathically instructs us without turning around, *"Do not dally."*

Sofia and I walk quickly and silently down the grey slab, crystal corridor holding hands. Shoulders pressed together, our stride is one.

"Do you think time passes slower or faster down here, or stays the same?"

"Maybe the same because it's still Earth?" I guess. "I am just keeping the faith that everything is perfect... remember Law of Attraction?"

No sooner than these words come out of Sofia's mouth, the crystal corridor opens to a huge expanse. We stop stunned.

"Oh mylanta ..." is what comes out of my mouth. "More like Atlan-tis!" Sofia gawks.

I can barely explain what I see. It is a huge expanse, like a gynormous crystal cavern with moss, grass, flowers, and some funny looking trees here and there. There are pyramids and pathways and shining lights coming from huge crystals as big as boulders, everywhere. Five large golden disks hover in the air and move about the huge underground cavern like hands on a clock. This 'courtyard' is as big as a city.

Little purple swirly flowers jut up through cracks in the slate floor and mountainous shards of crystal. Where the gray floor ends moss and tiny, short blades of grass begin to soften the land scape. Deep green fern like plants and tiny glowing mush- rooms intersperse with the funny flowers. The only other flora besides the swirly flowers, are orange and carnivorous looking. My suspicion is confirmed when I see one snap closed on a tiny flying bug.

"We keep the air clean," it tells me. "There would be bug clouds here without us!"

"Oh!" I exclaim. "Thank you!"

"You're thanking the plant aren't you?" Sofia asks. I nod. "It's keeping the air clean for us."

Sofia raises her eyebrows, "Great!"

The five moving gold discs shoot a lazer like light on us momentarily dazzling our sight. I shade my eyes, forgetting everything. I forget what we're doing here. I even forget my name for a minute. I am dazzled and scared.

As soon as I feel fear, there is movement by us. A stirring like the movement a propeller fan would make. A whirring noise and then... a being stands before us.

The being is long and tall with pale to translucent skin, white-yellow hair and ice blue eyes. It has arms, hands, feet and legs like a super skinny human. It looks kind of human, just taller and paler with larger eyes. It is wearing a white robe with a symbol on the chest.

It watches us expressionless and says nothing. Its eyes seem to look right through us. Goosebumps form all over my body.

Sofia grabs my hand and whispers, "Lena!" My name jolts me back to present.

"We are grateful to be here," I say.

"Grateful, yes. Good," says the being in a voice that is similar to the whirring of a fan with the depth of a very deep lake.

"Arghata is expecting us at the Galactic Round Table. Can you help us find it?" asks Sofia squeezing my hand.

"Think loving thoughts and think of the strength of our ancestors waiting for us above ground," she reminds me telepathically.

"Yes," I return telepathically. *"Thanks, girl."*

"Arghata is sending more human children to Council," the androgynous being buzzes in its whirring voice.

I can't tell whether it is male or female, maybe it's neither. Its features could be either and so could the voice. Trying to keep my thoughts on things I don't mind it knowing in case it too is telepathic, I think of love, of my Gram, Mom, Dad...even David.

"Yes, um... huuuummmm," I touch my throat hoping it turns blue with good communication energy. "We are Traveling Bridge Communicators...and this is our, our first day," is what comes out of my mouth.

"Travelers. First day. Surface Earth humor." The being moves instantly a measure of 1000 feet. It beckons us to follow with a slim, pale hand.

"Some of us do not trust surface humans," it says when we catch up. "Some of us prefer the Earth reset without humans."

"Oh! But we are peaceful. We took a vow to use our gifts for the good of all beings," Sofia tells the creature.

"Some humans do not keep promises, do not know trust," it says. "But Arghata is wise... Galactic Council is here."

The being extends its slim pale arm towards a shimmering silvery blue triangle door with deep purple gems lining the borders.

"You will be walking over to it now. "Thank you, friend," I say.

I think to Sofia, *"Let's get to this meeting and go home."*

The being, obviously telepathic too, says, "Yes, that is best. Attend meeting and return to surface." It whirs away leaving us.

I look back and scan the landscape not wanting to turn my back on it. I see it's pale face a half a mile away next to one of the smaller pyramids watching us.

I gulp, "Sofia, we have to stay positive while we are down here. Think of your favorite things. Do not think of anything scary, okay?"

"Believe me, I am doing that... thinking of all of our ancestors up there rooting for us, ya know?"

"Good. I'll think of that too." We approach the triangle. It slides open vertically from the center.

TWENTY-FOUR

This room is a pale blue crystal like celestite. Over one hundred beings seated at a large round table turn to look at us as we walk in. There is a kind of projector on the ceiling the shape of a white orb. It projects a spinning fourteen-point gold and silver star hologram on the shiny black round table below.

About thirty humans and beings that look kind of human with white gold hair and pale skin sit among mixed galaxy beings and elementals that are definitely not human. The luminosity about the sort of human ones is my only clue that they're not human.

The other beings include fish like creatures with whiskers and flat faces, blue skin and black eyes. There are grey beings shaped like aliens you see in movies, with cone shaped heads and long necks and fingers. There are several beings that look like cats, and several that resemble birds. A dozen or so Earth elementals with dark eyes like Arghata are also present.

Arghata waves to us and points to two open seats, "Welcome girls, sit here beside me."

Feeling super self-conscious, I look straight ahead at my seat and sit down. Trying to control my shaking hands, I fold them in my lap and look down at them in a tight little ball on my lap. I take a sip from the flask. The water, cool and silky, calms me enough to sit tall and look around.

Of the 30 or so humans, ten are close to our age, 15 to 16. Five are younger than us, like ten to 12. You can tell they are super smart though by their calm, focused expression. There are about ten humans in their twenties, several my parent's age, and a few could be grandparents. They all look very comfortable and that makes me feel much more stable. My shaking becomes less severe and I breathe a little deeper.

I notice the boy closest to my age sitting diagonal to me at the far end of the table, is the only one wearing Earth clothes. For that reason and because he's really cute, he stands out. Smiling directly at me, he pushes silky black hair behind an ear, and raises an eyebrow. He is pale, lean, and muscular. He leans in casually drumming his long fingers on the table, like he's at a hometown cafe waiting for his order.

I breathe deeply for the first time since I sat down and look away a light blush burning my cheeks. I am so happy to see a boy in Earth clothes, I could melt into a puddle. Maybe I won't change next time... if there is a next time.

The 14-point star symbol on the ceiling switches to an image of rotating Earth which projects on to the round table filling the entire surface area.

"Members of Galactic Council: Inner Earth Roundtable Chapter meet the newest traveling bridges, Lena Linnigan and Sofia Ounocanoa of North Carolina, United States of America."

Arghata stands behind us to make the announcement, placing a hand on my shoulder and a hand on Sofia's shoulder.

"Welcome," burbles a creature with blue skin like a seal, walrus like whiskers twitching as it sniffs the air in our direction.

"Thank you," we say in unison.

Some of the other beings nod and clap, a few send greetings to us telepathically in unfamiliar galactic languages.

A human girl close to our age, with shaved head on one side and long rainbow hair on the other side, wiggles her fingers at us. I notice she has a large raw crystal earring, a Herkimer diamond maybe, but no necklace. I touch my necklace asking telepathically, "Is that your power gem?"

She touches her earring and smiles, "Yes."

"Now," commands Arghata, in a thunderous rich tone. All eyes turn from us to her. "As all but the new girls know, the mission of Council is to assist Earth's ascension into the fifth dimension without wiping out the entire human race." She looks at us gravely thick brows knit together, full green lips in a terse straight line.

I gulp.

"At the current alarming rate of consumption and pollution of natural resources, and diseased human emotion, planet Earth must purify daily with extreme weather. She will continue sending her messengers, the elements to cleanse toxic low vibrations of humans and half breeds with hurricanes, wildfire, tornados, tsunamis, and floods in order to raise the vibration enough to enter the fifth dimension...because she must.

It is then up to us, members of Council, to work with Earth and her messengers to ensure a smooth transition into 5D... before all of surface humanity becomes extinct."

The spinning Earth projection on the round table turns into a detailed map of Earth seen from space pinpointing recent extreme weather sites in red.

"The course of action for those who are new and as a reminder to us all. First, recalibrate humans and half breeds in power to be in harmonious alignment with ascension by raising their vibration with light and sound so we can *all* enter the fifth dimension with New Earth. Second, preserve and revive what's left of Earth's natural resources namely water, air, and land so surface life will thrive rather than weaken in the new position.

In the meantime, our dear Mother Earth, will continue sending extreme weather to purify low energy areas... and the raptor race will continue to use half breeds to consume and pollute the planet, weakening the human species until they are completely fearful and under control."

The words *Mission: New Earth Advanced Recalibration* in just about every human language I've ever seen scrolls across the table. Galactic languages follow.

A slender blue birdlike being with a beak and black marble eyes stands. His throat center swirls blue as he communicates the following telepathically, "To fill you in further, Lena and Sofia from North Carolina... Consider the old seven-chakra system. Are you familiar with this?"

"Yes," I confirm.

"Kind of," Sofia admits.

The image on the roundtable switches to a person seated in yoga easy pose with seven colorful chakras red root chakra, orange creativity chakra, yellow power center chakra, green heart chakra, turquoise throat chakra, dark blue third eye chakra, and purple crown chakra.

"Old 3D Earth was vibrating at the third chakra, the Manipura chakra, navel level, which is the seat of power. Therefore wars, lust, aggression, and greed were common. New 5D Earth will vibrate at fifth chakra level, the Vishudda or throat Chakra. This new vibration is about speaking your truth and moving away from low vibration thoughts and actions. Humans need to be recalibrated to vibrate at this higher frequency, this higher vibration to align and ascend with Earth. Does this make sense?"

"Yes, totally," I say a bit loudly, excited that I am finally starting to get it.

Galactic laughter of many different pitches like singing bowls surrounds the room. The boy in Earth clothes laughs the loudest with a voice so rich and strong, I am happy to have heard it.

The birdlike being continues, "More than half of humans and half breeds on surface Earth are greedy, lustful, violent, and fearful. These emotions carry extremely toxic low vibrations which spread like cancer preventing Earth's full ascension. We need to raise the overall surface frequency in order for humanity to survive the ascension.

Once we have a handle on raising the vibration of human species, birth rate must slow, consumption of natural resources must be cut, and love and gratitude must reign. Otherwise Earth's purification process, extreme weather and natural disas- ter, will result in the extinction of the human race just like the extinction of the many animals, birds, and sea creatures... you have seen already."

"Very good summation, Thal. The young ones have under- stood every word. Thank you," Arghata touches her heart, nodding at the blue green birdlike being. Thal bows and his swirling blue throat center fades as he takes his seat.

I raise my hand. Arghata gestures for me to stand.

"What is a half-breed and how do you know if someone is one?" I ask quickly then sit down.

The image on the table changes to a split screen with a human male on one side and a lizard looking creature on the other side.

"A half breed," bellows Argahata, spittle flying out of her mouth, "is a cross between a raptor and a human. Raptors are the one race working against us to keep Earth from ascending. They wish to consume all of Earth's natural resources and enslave the human species using mind control methods. You can tell humans are half-breeds by their desire for money and power. Anytime a human in power is bent on consuming and polluting as much of Earth's resources as he or she can like water, forests, oil, land, there is a great chance that he or she is either a half breed or ... a pure raptor. The raptor planet vibrates at a low level as well and this acid environment is their comfort zone, war, lust, control...it is most unpleasant. But let us stop here to avoid information overload."

A golden feline creature stands. She has amber cat like eyes, short cat ears on top of her head, and thick golden hair like a lion's mane falling over one eye and down her back. Leaning forward with her arms on the table, she looks around and sniffs. Her long whiskers twitch from side to side.

"Who among us has powerful humans in their immediate family...someone that works... in a large corporation associated with... polluting or degrading water? I sense there is someone here."

Heart pounding I look around, hoping someone else will stand. When no one does, I push my chair back and stand with wobbly knees. "I do."

"Lena Linnigan of Wilmington, North Carolina, the area of the recent hurricane and oil spill, where water is too polluted to drink. Please show us the current state of the area."

The image of Earth turns and zooms into North Carolina, then zooms into the coastline of Wrightsville Beach. The ocean is black for miles. Sea creatures lay in piles of dead and dying along the beach.

"Please show us the river that was the drinking water source," lion lady says. The image zooms to the Cape Fear River, a sad brown thing snaking towards the black ocean.

"Now, tell us Lena," says lion lady nodding to me, "about ... the family member associated with water."

Suddenly my throat is so dry I can't speak. I take a sip of water and look at Sofia, Arghata and the boy in Earth clothes briefly for support.

"Okay... my um, my father is a lawyer. He defends big businesses... the chemical company that's been ah polluting the Cape Fear River forever is one of his clients. He also invests with oil companies. H-his mother's family is uh from a long line of big business people who pretty much only care about money. He um thinks he can make a buck... I mean make a lot of money off the water crisis."

I look around at the rainbow of colored faces staring at me. No one seems surprised or angry just supportive and understanding.

"And there is someone else. I smell... another. Tell us about...him," says lion lady.

"You mean my Uncle Leo," I say shifting my feet and sticking my hands in the webby pockets. "That's my Dad's brother. He makes commercials in uh Hollywood, California. He's so rich he *owns* an island. He says people with money don't

have to worry about water or other resources running out because they can buy whatever they want."

I shrug and look around. Sweat drips secretly from my armpits in the webby galactic outfit and I wish I could sit down.

"Please continue," says Arghata.

The boy in Earth clothes winks at me and says telepathically,

"Relax. This questioning is normal and you're doing great!"
"Thanks," I return telepathically, grateful for the support.

"So my Uncle Leo and... my um my Dad... want me to do a commercial for their new investment, because uh I am an actress ... I mean it's a skill I have. They're investing in a water substitute... a product called Wüter because they would rather make money off the water crisis than help pay to clean up Earth water. They think that Wüter is going to be a really big deal," I finish biting my bottom lip embarrassed and feeling sort of guilty.

"We know about Wüter," a grey purple birdlike being emits staring deeply into my eyes. "And you are going to do what your father and uncle wish?"

"I, well yes, I'm uh ... I'm going to Los Angeles Friday to be in this live news commercial or something. I'm supposed to tell people how much I love Wüter! But I tried it and I don't like it! I would rather keep Earth water clean! A water substitute is scary!"

I start to shake and try to hold back the tears building behind my eyes. One tear escapes from each eye sliding down my cheeks into my mouth. I taste the salt before blotting the tear stain off my cheeks with shaky fingertips.

"Thank you, Lena. You may sit down," says Arghata.

Sniffling and shaky, I sit down and take a sip of water from my flask. Sofia reaches for my hand under the table and gives it a squeeze. I squeeze back.

The image of North Carolina zooms back out to a view of Earth from space. Red lights on the map show where water on Earth is too polluted for human consumption.

"These are the areas on Earth where the water is already too polluted to drink," says a twelve-ish year old Chinese girl. "At this rate, by 2050, less than 10% of the water on Earth will be suitable for human consumption. Without pure water there will be no life left on the surface of Earth. The water substitute they ask you to put your face on, like pharmaceuticals and Genetically Modified foods will weaken the life force so severely, even without extreme weather, humans will die off. Only the wealthy will have access to pure water and they will not last long."

"Uh my Mom suggested I use the money I make from the commercial to launch a water clean-up," I say hopefully.

"Yes, good. We revisit this next time. The important point today is your father and uncle. You must bring them to Inner Earth for recalibration. We will reset and align their alliance vibration to the ascension plan. Right now they are vibrating on raptor greed level, unconsciously working towards the extinction of humanity, and the total destruction of Earth's natural resources."

"Bring them down here?" "For recalibration." "How will I do that?"

"You will know when the time comes. You are here because of your ability to tap into Universal Consciousness. Remember this and the power in your lineage and never be confused as to how to achieve. Just know it will happen and allow it to unfold."

"Will recalibration hurt?"

"It will be the best thing that ever happens to them. When they leave they will feel perfectly at peace...as though they had a spa weekend. They will then *help you* launch the clean water project. This is part of the ascension plan, raise the vibration of people in power first, especially the half-breeds. We begin with the people closest to us and spiral out."

The boy in Earth clothes shifts in his chair. I look at him. *"Don't worry,"* he says telepathically. *"Your family will be fine. I had to bring my father in too. He is a better person now and doesn't remember a thing."*

"Thank you," I return telepathically trying to smile.

A lady in a white robe with white gold hair speaks next, "Everyone get comfortable. The following information will arrive through theta waves in the form of sound and light. We are about to receive attunement with New Earth so relax and enjoy."

The Earth map disappears and soft pink, blue and green lights replace it filling the room. Vibrational sound follows. Low, steady, deep beats alternating with quick higher pitched beats and an instrument that sounds like a harp. I feel it throughout my body and mind. I close my eyes and receive the knowledge. Ten, twenty, maybe thirty minutes pass. The light and sound fades then stop.

No one moves or speaks for another ten minutes while we absorb what feels like healing, health, strength, happiness, and joy.

Finally, the Earth map reappears and the words, *"Council is adjourned,"* slide across the screen in thousands of human and galactic languages.

Like ninety percent of the beings disappear instantly sending telepathic good byes, thank you, pleased to meet you, welcome to the mission, see you next time, and congratulations girls.

I send the words and feelings of, "thank you" and "good to meet you," back to all.

When Sofia, Arghata, the boy in Earth clothes, the rainbow haired Earth girl, a white gold lady in a robe, the fish looking being, lion lady, and me are the only ones left at the roundtable, I let out a very deep sigh. The fourteen point star image appears once again on the surface of the table, this time spinning gold and silver and blue.

"We are here for you, Lena from North Carolina," says Lion Lady. "I am Mirinayana, beings who know me call me Miri. You will do well in your assignment... I smell the victory already."

"Thank you, Miri," I say wanting to touch her mane. Miri smiles, emits a very subtle purr, and teleports out of the room.

"We all share strength here so you will never be without that," says the fish being without introducing himself before walking over to the control board at the head of the table.

"You did great and you will do great," says the boy in Earth clothes shaking my hand. "I'm Denali. I was born in China but we live in BC now. My father is a state politician and boy did he need that recalibration."

"That's reassuring. I do love my father even if he is on the wrong side," I say still shaking Denali's strong, cool hand.

When I realize we've been shaking hands for much longer than normal and beings are starting to stare at us, I remove my hand from his, blushing.

He smiles again and the warmth of his smile makes all my chakras spin. I've never felt a connection with a guy like this before.

While Denali is shaking Sofia's hand I get a really good look

at him. He is slim, tall but not too tall, and wiry lean with silky black hair that keeps falling over his left eye. His dark eyes slant slightly towards a perfectly straight nose. I don't see any power gems on his ears or neck and then...I see it...a black onyx pinky ring on his left hand. It is raised in a silver band and fits him perfectly.

The Earth clothes he's wearing denote a laid back, some- what rebellious persona, grey jeans, a black tee shirt that compliment his pale skin, and black and white with orange detail high top sneakers.

He notices me drinking him in and winks. I blush hard and look away biting my lip. I have never been good at flirting. Astrologically speaking it's because I have Saturn conjunct Venus in my fifth house of romance and fun.

"You did excellent today, girls. We are happy to have you on the team," Arghata says.

"Lena knows her part of the mission now but what about me?" Sofia asks.

"Your time will come, Sofia. Just having you with us is enough for now."

"Arghata, we have important business to discuss," burbles the fish being.

"That we do, Qi," she affirms then turning to us, "It is time

to go back to the surface, girls. We will see you soon. Stay healthy, strong, and clear and be ready to receive messages from elementals and animal messengers as needed."

"Nice to meet you both," says Denali. "Feel free to reach out anytime. "I know what it's like to be on a first mission, Lena and I am happy to... I want to help any way I can. So, reach out! I mean that." Denali teleports out, leaving his warm smile stamped in my mind.

"How do we get back to the surface?" asks Sofia.

Arghata laughs, "The same way you came in! Hold on to your pendants, really that's just a beginner's tool, but it works. Think of the circle you made. Imagine being there and that's it!"

Closing my eyes to concentrate on the transfer, I hear Arghata laughing, a rumbling melodic thing with a violin like backbone. In an instant we are back in the stone circle above ground.

TWENTY-FIVE

Back on the surface, a sea of ancestors surrounds us, Gram among them. "Lena, my own blood and Sofia, my dearest friend's blood!! Congratulations! Your first inter-dimensional traveling experience was quite a success."

"Thank you, Gram!" I say. "Thank you!" Sofia yells.

Gram's spirit essence hugs us. Her hug feels like a fluttering of tiny warm bees wings mixed with static electricity. I am so tired. I just want to melt on the ground and take a nap right here but adrenaline keeps me upright. I sway slightly with the effort.

"As much as I would love to stay and continue the celebration, we need to close the circle. Your ride will be here in one hour. That means you must run down the mountain," instructs Gram.

"Run?" I moan.

"Closing circle, everybody!" Gram announces authoritatively.

The hooting and hollering stops, bodies and light energies press in.

"These young women, the youngest in our family lines, Lena Linnigan my own dear grand-daughter and Sofia Ounacouna, my great friend's grand-daughter," she says voice catching, pride dripping from every word. "Have had great success today! They have made their first trip into fifth dimension, received a power pendant, and ...they have taken seats at Galactic Council."

A peach glow takes over her essence, turquoise electric currents burst like tiny bubbles where her heart would be. Is that what pride looks like energetically?

"Our girls, Lena and Sofia have begun their life destiny here today at Earth Vortex ...and they have proven that, in a time of great need, our lineage remains strong! This is a day we remember forever! It is a sacred and joyous occasion. We honor you!"

Ancestors, light beings, and elementals join together and send up a celebratory roar that shakes the Earth, "We honor you!"

I feel the love and strength of ancestors deep in my bones and blood. It is so good I wish I could keep that feeling forever.

I must look exhausted though because Gram says, "Go home and rest! Rest and rebuild strength. Think of Earth Vortex as your grounding place of power. Come here whenever you need stability and strength for as long or as short a time as you like."

Drumming, humming, hooting and hollering and then Sofia begins to sing.

"The next generation of bridges has come to speak with Mother

Earth. The next generation of bridges is here to take our place in line.

Behold our generation, we are that generation! The next generation of bridges has come to speak for Mother Earth!"

I sing the next two rounds with her for a total of three rounds of the Earth power song. When the third round is over, the ancestors turn back into dust and mica and sink into the ground.

We close our eyes.

I don't know why, we just do.

We sit for a few minutes until the little stream is the loudest thing in the forest again.

When we open our eyes, Smokey is with us. Sofia pats him on the head. I drink the remainder of my water in one thirsty gulp and we begin the descent down the mountain.

TWENTY-SIX

The ride back to Daffodil House is a blur. I barely remember thanking Aunt Laurie or handing Sofia her book. But somehow I end up home. Mom is upstairs in her office and nothing is cooking, so no dinner tonight which is fine by me.

I toss my backpack on the table and plunge into the fridge to make whatever looks good. David sneaks up behind me pulling out my bun, still wet from the little stream.

"Where did you go today dorkina Lena? Did you have a nice hike with your little friend?" he snickers an I-am-programmed-to-tease-my-sister-laugh.

I know it well.

"Oh my gosh, David, is that really you? Or is this a mirage of you?" I ask in mock surprise waving my arms in his direction. "I am amazed you are out of your room. But since you are and are actually talking to me, I assume you want something so what is it?" I snap.

I am not in the mood to be patient. I want to be left alone.

I twist my hair back up into a bun and put lunchmeat, cheese, bread, lettuce and cucumber on the table. The cutting board is next to the sink and I grab that too. I wash my hands and David stands there looking like a sad puppy that's just been smacked on the butt with a newspaper. He is so helpless in the kitchen.

I sigh. "Do you want a sandwich, David?"

"If you're making one for yourself, sure." He shuffles his feet and shoves his hands in his short pockets. "How about turkey and cheese with mustard?"

"Fine. I will make you a sandwich." I grab two plates then rinse and cut the lettuce and cucumber for mine.

"Nothing green on mine, please."

"Fine." I make David's plain old turkey and cheese on wheat with mustard first to get him out of my hair. Of all nights for him to be talkative, he's gotta pick tonight. "Here," I hand him the sandwich on a plate.

He dumps chips on it, grabs a paper towel and starts to head out, then changes his mind and says, "So do you like your new friend?"

Why is he so interested in what I am doing tonight?

"Yes, David. I do. She is awesome and yea, we went for a hike with her dog today. It was fun."

I stand with my hands on my hips. *"David I made you a sand-wich that's about as loving as I can be, tonight, I am tired. Please go away,"* I say in my mind broadcasting those feelings with my eyes.

"Oh, nice. Well, thanks for the sandwich," he turns with a shrug and puppy dog eyes padding on bare feet back to his room.

I feel sorry for David. He's gotta be depressed here without

the ocean and his surf buddies. But hey, at least I made him a sandwich so he won't starve.

I put cucumber and lettuce on my sandwich then go out to the front porch and sit on the swing. I sit there for an hour doing nothing just watching the birds and squirrels, thinking, and taking tiny bites of my sandwich.

At some point Mom comes out and talks to me. She asks me how my hike was I say fine. Asks me where I got the necklace, I say it was a present from Sofia. Asks me some other stuff and then leaves. I sit on the swing and do nothing for an hour longer then head upstairs. It is only 8:30pm but I am ready for bed. I need sleep.

There is a wooden jewelry box on my bureau that Pop made and later I had my favorite poem inscribed on the top. I put the pendant in there and close the lid.

I sit on a pillow on the floor for quiet time. Thoughts come rushing into my mind from every direction. Thoughts come and go and I watch them. Finally, I feel somewhat clear and get up. Mom must have closed my window again. I open it and fresh air pours into my room. I close the air conditioner vent and turn on my fan. I climb into bed, asleep in seconds.

TWENTY-SEVEN

When I wake up I am disoriented and groggy. Mom is standing above me looking concerned. Great.

"What time is it?" "Almost dinner time." "What?" I blink.

Mom sits on the edge of my bed. "You slept over twenty hours. Maybe you're overexerting yourself with the bike rides and hikes. You seemed pretty out of it when I talked to you on the porch last night too."

"Maybe. It was a long hike..."

She puts a cool hand on my forehead.

"You don't have a fever. Stick out your tongue for me."

"Mo-om, I feel fine!" I roll my eyes but stick out my tongue anyway.

"Your throat and tonsils look healthy. Just take it easy tonight and tomorrow, okay? You need to be rested for Friday.

You fly at 6am for your first commercial ever! Are you excited?" Mom smoothes my hair and kisses my forehead.

"I don't even know what I am saying yet. They didn't send my lines or anything."

"Dad said it's short and sweet, you know commercials.

They're usually only a few lines."

I don't saying anything more about it.

"We're having pizza and salad tonight, from that new place, Salina's. Are you hungry." Mom wrinkles her forehead. "You're not doing drugs are you? You know you can talk to me about anything?"

"Oh my gosh, Mom!" I erupt. "I would never do drugs. That makes people stupid! I cannot believe you just asked me that."

I jump out of bed and give Mom the-what-are-you-even-talking-about-look. Then walk down the hall to my bathroom. Mom follows me.

"Mother, stop following me. I just needed the extra sleep I guess. I was tired. I hiked all day yesterday like straight up a mountain without stopping." I eye her impatiently while applying toothpaste to my toothbrush.

"I believe you. Just don't think because I'm writing my book that I am not paying attention to your life and what you do, okay?"

I start brushing my teeth and Mom smoothes my hair again. Why is she always touching my hair? It's annoying. I exhale and inhale deeply. Be calm, Lena, she means well. I smile a mouth full of toothpaste foam and take my mother's hands in mine.

I look her in the eye, "I would tell you if anything is wrong but I'm fine. I'm just having fun showing my new friend around. She's never been anywhere but Montana and Idaho."

"Those are two states I have never been," says Mom.

"Me too and apparently they are way different than here. People drive like speed demons in Montana! Did you know that?"

"I have heard people say that, yes. Where did you girls hike?"

"Around the Crystal Caves."

"Is that where your father found the emeralds?"

"Yep," I rinse, spit and smile in the mirror. I like my teeth. It took me awhile to get used to how big they looked after the braces came off but now I like them. Bent over the sink rinsing my face in cold water, I see Mom start to leave out the corner of my eye.

I stop her before she walks out of the bathroom, "Listen, Mom! I want you to know I will never do drugs or get drunk, mmkay. I am not even interested in those things. Chocolate and espresso are more than enough for me. I can hardly handle that!"

Mom smiles. "I believe you. I'm only doing my part to stay in the loop."

"And...Sofia would never do that stuff either. Her Mom

messed up like that like abusing pharmaceuticals and Sofia is pissed at her like you wouldn't believe."

"Please don't use the word pissed."

"She is extremely angry and disappointed with her mother then. Happy?"

"I'm sorry she has to deal with that. Thank you for telling me."

Ding Dong. The doorbell. "Pizza's here!"

Mom hands me a towel to dry my face. No wonder I worry

about everything! Mom is totally passing that gene down to me. The worry gene.

Chicken with pesto and artichoke on one half and pepperoni and red sauce on the other half of our pizza. That and a huge salad is what we have for dinner. I am starving and eat three chicken pesto slices. David of course eats pepperoni.

If Arghata and the rest of the round table could see me now, eating pizza with my family in a Daffodil Yellow suburban house finally starting to feel somewhat normal again.

The low Earth rumble alert sounds in my ear. A message already?

How am I supposed to get it with Mom and David around?

I eat my salad and clean up, thanking Mom for dinner and excusing myself to go for a walk.

A fawn kneels on the lawn half hidden by the nearest rose bush. The fawn has white spots on its back and a white stripe down its nose. When I am within two feet of her, she fixes large, calm black eyes on me and I receive this message tele- pathically. It's a dictated recording of Arghata's voice:

"Begin diet and exercise recommendation message. To be successful in your mission, you must build strength. Do this by exercising daily and alternating between kinds of exercise. Walk, bike, hike, jog, do push ups and sit ups, swim, lift weights, do martial arts; some form of exercise every day linking movement to breath.

You will also need to increase your flexibility. Yoga is great for that. Rest when you need to.

Expect the sleep cycle following inter-dimensional travel to be twice as long for cellular regeneration. Sleeping 18-24 hours is not unusual.

Eat mostly plant foods also known as fruits and vegetables, raw, lightly steamed or cooked in soups. Eat some meat, fish, cheese, and eggs to build stamina, local or wild when possible and always say a blessing to the animal it came from before eating it.

Some sugar and caffeine is fine no more than 1-2 portions a day, take it before exercise to make the most of your routine. Good luck! Message complete."

The fawn stands, eats one yellow rose, then scampers across the street.

An animal messenger?! The animals are in on it too then.

So I need to exercise. Okay. I do that anyway, Ill just amp it up a little and get super strong.

"Hey, fawn," I think to the memory of it's pretty face. *"We're on the same team! Thanks for the message!"*

Sofia's face pushes the fawn's memory out of my mind and I see her in her room looking glum. She's sitting at her desk staring at a picture of her mom. I decide to walk over and see how she is doing.

TWENTY-EIGHT

Bark one, bark two, bark three.

Smokey is in the yard excited to see me, wagging his stub tail. I let myself in the gate and pet him. He follows me to the front door. I knock and Sofia's little sister answers.

"Hi," she says. "I know you."

"Yep, you're sister and I are friends now so I am not a stranger anymore. I'm Lena," I say extending my hand.

"I'm Tabatha. Peoples who know me call me Tab."

Tabatha's hair is just as wild and curly as Sofia's. Like last time, she's got residual mixed media art on her face, and something shimmery stuck to her foot. She doesn't shake my hand just looks at it so I pat the top of her head.

"Hey, don't pet me!" she squeals running backwards a yard on her tiptoes like a football player. She dances a little in her irritation her blue knee length nightgown twirling at the bottom, "Why does everyone twy to pet me!!! I am not a dog! Ugh!"

"Okay, okay!" I laugh. "I wont pet you. I just like your hair is all. You and your sisters... is she here?"

"She's in her bedwoom. But you can't go back there wight now. She's in twouble."

"Trouble? For what?"

"She swept all day and didn't do her chores." "Oh man!" I say.

"So she is gwounding for the night and can't come out." "Uhhm, is your Dad or Aunt here then?"

"Daddy's still at wook. But Aunty's here...watching TV. Auntyyyyy!!!!" Tabatha yells into the house.

Aunt Laurie comes to the door and folds her arms across her chest, "Hi Lena."

"Hi!" I smile assessing her level of anger at Sofia as mild. "I wanted to see how Sofia's doing but Tab says she is grounded for sleeping all day. Just so you know I slept all day too..."

"Oh you did, huh?"

"Ya, I think its because we hiked for so long into high alti- tude and didn't drink enough water. My mom was concerned too. I slept til 5:30!"

"Dehydration? I didn't think of that. You gotta make sure to replace those electrolytes and drink enough water or sport drinks with potassium when you're sweating. When I played basketball in college, we drank a ton of water and sports drinks. It's just part of the game."

"I knew you played basketball," I say tapping her on the arm like an old pal or something. "What college did you go to?"

Aunt Laurie laughs, "Montana State." She smiles and her eyes soften. "I would probably be coaching now but these girls need a mom figure. I can be a little hard on them because I

don't want them turning out like," she looks down at Tabatha and mouths, "their mom."

I nod, "Sofia told me. She's mad at," I mouth, "her mom too.

So I know she wouldn't do that... I mean turn out like that." Aunt Laurie looks at my face measuring my trustworthiness. "They are good kids. Okay. She can come out for a few but she can't go anywhere tonight...Sofia!" She turns and yells into the house. "Lena is here!"

Sofia appears barefoot in a long purple blue maxi dress, the kind that hits your ankle. Tabatha and Aunt Laurie go back into the house. Sofia joins me on the porch shutting the door behind her. We sit on the steps. Smokey sits between us. I put my arm around him and pat his broad chest.

"He likes you," Sofia says sounding not so happy about it.

"I like him," I say. "I heard you slept all day," I give her a knowing look. "I told your Aunt I slept all day too and I think it's because we were hiking in high altitude and didn't drink enough water."

"Which is true. We probably shoulda drank more water." Sofia says flicking a pebble off the porch. "Thanks."

"We'll need to think of a cover for sleeping longer next time we travel so we don't get into trouble again."

"Did *you* get in trouble?"

"No, but my Mom was worrying and asking me a thousand questions."

"So why are you saying we? *You* didn't get grounded." Sofia finds another pebble to flick off the porch.

I shrug. "Did you get the dietary and exercise message yet?" "No, what message?" Sofia scowls impatient, not like her normal self.

"We uh, we need to exercise daily. We should alternate between kinds of exercise...and do yoga or some basic stretching too. We need to eat lots of fruits and vegetables, some local or wild meat is okay as long as you thank the animal before eating it. Sugar and caffeine in small doses only like...Oh and expect to sleep twice as long after traveling."

Sofia listens but looks irritated. I've never seen her like this! I continue feeling slightly wounded with a little waver in my voice.

"She sent me a fawn messenger."

"Really? A fawn? Awww, I guess I didn't get one because I was stuck inside," for a minute her eyes go soft and she smiles. "What are we gonna say next time about sleeping?"

"I don't know yet but maybe we can sleep in the yard again or something."

"Okay on the exercise" Sofia says. "I bike and walk a lot so that's easy. "I do need to stretch more. I've never done yoga...Maybe you can teach me?"

"Sure. I can teach you the basics like sun salutations. I've been taking classes since I was twelve. We have yoga at my school. I do it three nights a week. The only part I don't like is when they do the Om."

Sofia snorts disdainfully, "I've seen that on commercials and in movies. Why do they do that?"

"Om? It's like the sound the crown chakra makes or something... like the throat chakra makes the hum sound and is blue. Om is dark purple...Not all teachers do it... I mean it's not mandatory."

"You and your sun and moon signs and yoga classes," Sofia grumbles looking at her feet. "You're so. new age coastal." She puts her head in her lap and wraps her arms around her legs burying her face in the soft folds of her maxi dress.

"You're kind of a grouch today," I say. She groans.

"Sorry. I always get like this a week before my moon comes. Plus I am grounded for the night so that doesn't help," she mumbles into her legs.

"Oh, I get that too."

"Seriously. It's like I am totally fine one day then the next day, bam, I am sad and grouchy. Then a week later my moon comes.

Aunty says I should start writing my sad days and moon days on the calendar because then I wont be surprised when it comes."

"Sounds like a good idea."

"Hopefully, I'll get used to it one day. Sorry I'm a grouch."

"Hey! I get it. Thanks for telling me. Well um, mind if I take Smokey for a walk then?"

Smokey knows the word "walk" and begins wagging his tail and doing a little prance. I have to laugh.

"Sure. He would love that. I'll get the leash," Sofia goes inside and brings his leash and two plastic bags out. "When you get back, put him the yard and leave the leash on the front porch, okay? I'm gonna do my chores. Maybe Ill see you tomorrow."

"I'm flying to LA tomorrow to do that Wüter commercial. So I wont see you. Did you get the download of how I have to... how I'm supposed to," I lower my voice to a whisper, "bring my dad and uncle in for recalibration?"

"No. I didn't. Mine was something about my mom."

"Your mom? What?"

"I don't wanna talk about it right now. Maybe another time..." She turns to walk up the steps than twists back around. "You like that dude, Denali, don't you? I saw the way you looked at him. It was pretty obvious."

"What?" I squeal embarrassed and caught off guard.

"He was the only one wearing normal clothes is all and it was cool… that he didn't change. He just came how he was. I like that."

"He does seem cool. You're allowed to like him."

When I don't say anything else about it Sofia goes inside for Smokey's leash. I stand there thinking of Denali's smile and silky black hair, the touch of his hand.

Wow. I do like him.

Sofia leashes Smokey when she comes back out and hands him over to me for the walk. "If you need me tomorrow, message me, alright?"

"I will. Thanks. Wish you could come."

"You'll be fine, girl. I have faith in you. Since I met you like my entire world has changed. You are a powerful person whether you know it or not."

Sofia gives me a hug. She smells clean and citrusy like oranges and grapefruit. Her curly hair tickles my nose.

Smokey barks an impatient whine bark. He is ready to walk.

"Love you, girl," I tell Sofia.

"Love you too."

TWENTY-NINE

Friday morning 4:44AM, Mom and I are standing outside of Raleigh Durham International Airport at American Air departures.

My crystal quartz power pendant is tucked safely beneath a light peach sweater. Sage green shorts and like bone colored strappy sandals color coordinate perfectly with the peach of my sweater and vegan nail polish. I pull on my backpack and mom sets the little roller suitcase in front of me. It wobbles and I catch it before it falls.

"As soon as you land, text your father. He'll be there when you get off the plane. If he's not for any reason call me and Ill stay with you until you see him, okay?"

"Yes, Mom."

We've been over this a half dozen times.

"Make Uncle Leo take you shopping while you're there and...try to get a head shot."

I nod.

Mom squeezes my shoulders, "My little girl off to Holly- wood! I'm so proud of you!" she says starting to get emotional.

"Thanks, Mom."

"Have a great time out there!" She hugs me and kisses me on the cheek. I walk in through the turnstile wheeling my luggage behind me. Mom blows me another kiss when I am inside and I wave goodbye.

I SLEEP HEAVILY the entire flight and wake up to a stewardess shaking my shoulder.

"Naptime's over, girlfriend! You're in LA... time to get off."

"Ahhhh...thanks. Sorry," I mumble startled.

Being a bridge makes me sleep like a log. I toss my backpack over my shoulders and collect my suitcase before ambling out, the last one off. Dad is waiting for me as planned.

"There's my girl!" he booms enveloping me in a bear hug which instantly evolves into steering me towards the exit.

FOUR HOURS LATER, I am in a makeup chair rehearsing my three lines. A slim, excitable guy with turquoise eyebrows hums as he trims and styles my hair.

"Wüter is refreshing. It's got minerals and tastes like real water. I drink it when Earth water is not available and during restrictions so I can take longer showers."

Not very interesting for sure and also I am lying, which I don't like. But if I use the money to launch a clean water

project, that makes it okay, right? Like that saying, 'the end justifies the means.'

Plus I have to get Dad and Uncle Leo in for recalibration.

How am I supposed to do all of this? I have no plan.

Feeling like I'm in a pressure cooker, looking out, I start to sweat. My breathing gets ragged. What did Arghata say to do when I don't know how I'll do something? Give over to universal flow? What exactly does that mean?

The guy with the turquoise eyebrows is yacking away about something but all I can see is a pair of turquoise eyebrows floating in space. Where is his face? Shoot! I cannot have a panic attack right now!

Fight, Lena! Fight to stay here! I touch my pendant and close my eyes looking for the strength everyone tells me I have.

When the makeup artist, Ally, a pretty lady with bright blue eyes touches my cheek, I sense that she is a Star Seed too. Her presence calms me enough to say, "Please don't take this personally but I don't wanna talk right now. I need to meditate before I go on set."

"You do you and I'll do me, how's that sound!" she winks at me. "It's no problem...and by the way I love your necklace!"

"Thank you," I say closing my eyes as she begins matching foundation to my skin tone. Then, I call to Gram telepathically for advice.

"Gram, I'm in Hollywood. We're about to do the Wüter commercial. I don't know if I am doing the right thing and I'm anxious. Please help?"

"Hi honey. I know what you mean. Lying is not good energy. But your mission to recalibrate your father and uncle to Earth's ascension comes first. Once they are re-calibrated they will have different ideas about Wüter and Earth water."

"You mean like once they're recalibrated they'll want to help clean Earth water and stop being greedy, right?"

"Exactly."

"So how do I do it? How do I get them in for recalibration?"

"I don't have the answer to that grand daughter. It is something for you to figure out yourself. This is your life and your mission. Have faith and go with the flow. Take the best opportunity. The Universe has your back."

I breathe out a loud mouth breath and Ally, the makeup artist laughs a sparkly laugh, "Ten more minutes and you'll be outta this chair. Can you make it?"

If makeup was my biggest worry, I'd be in good shape. I laugh and it melts away the top layer of tension.

THIRTY

I am surprised when I see a half dozen teenagers file into the newsroom behind the politicians. I had my own suite to get ready in because I am Uncle Leo's niece so I didn't see any of them earlier. I walk in from the opposite end alone swiveling my head like an owl. This place is huge!

I haven't seen Uncle Leo once yet and it's making me worry all the more about my mission. Plus they made me take the power pendant off when they outfitted me in a forest green top and white jeans.

"Twenty minutes!" the production guy yells.

As everyone is taking their seats and getting microphones adjusted, intuition tells me I absolutely must have my pendant. Turning on a dime like an Olympic ice skater, I push past surprised people in the hallway and sprint to my dressing room.

"Wrong way!" a lady in fashionable glasses says sternly, holding her clip board in front of me, trying to block my passage and corral me back to the studio.

"I left something important in my dressing room! I'll be two seconds!"

"You have thirty seconds to be on the set or I will come looking for you," she says harshly. "You're Leo's niece, right?"

"Yes!" I yell pushing past her. "And I need my lucky pendant!"

"Do not add anything to your outfit! It was carefully selected!"

Throwing the dressing room door open, I lunge for my back-pack and jam the pendant into my pocket. I'm already heading back to the set when her frowning face meets me in the doorway.

"Going to the set now!" I yell over my shoulder.

"You're so special because you're the boss's niece..." I hear her mutter under her breath, high fashion heels clacking down the hall.

Back on set, everyone is seated practicing lines. A stagehand comes over and puts a tiny microphone on my collar and someone from makeup dusts a little powder on my forehead as soon as I sit down.

Out of the blue, fire element sounds an alert warning in my ear.

"Crackle, hiss! *Wildfire is heading your way. The area you are in is due for purification.*"

Ohmygosh! A fire!? Now?

Will I have time to do this?

Can I do this?

Can I freaking do this?

Do I have a choice? How long do I have? Omygosh? Omygosh!

Right on cue though, as in divine timing, Dad and Uncle Leo walk in and sit down in the front row of the live audience. They wave and I wave back. I swallow the huge lump forming in my throat. I need to be able to speak.

I mentally call to Sofia for support. *"Sof! I'm in Los Angeles, a wildfire is on the way and I still have to get my dad and uncle in for recalibration. I am scared...stiff!"*

Nothing but crickets for two full minutes then, *"Guurrrrllll,"* comes Sofia's voice. *"You were born to do this. You have your pendant?"*

"Yes."

"Sending you strength and love! I picked out my bike!"

"Funny. Thanks. I love you!"

"I love you, gurl."

"Ten minutes," the director yells.

Set lights and a big screen behind us flashes on, *Channel Four News.*

"Turn your place cards to the audience please," the director yells.

We do and I see who everyone is and where they're from. My place card says, Lena Linnigan, Wilmington, North Carolina.

The lady across from me is Senator Paula Planco, New York, New York. Next to her is Senator Arthur Bunk, Houston, Texas. The teen girl next to me is Sandy Roobios, Phoenix, Arizona. The boy next to her is Philip Hostettler, San Diego, California. Beside Philip is Bai Zhao from Hong Kong, China and Albert Cho from Taipei, Taiwan. There is also Aurora Yazzie from Juneau, Alaska and Amoli Patel from New Delhi, India and so on.

Next to our place cards there are two clear plastic bottles, labeled A and B. I am guessing they're water and Wüter, maybe a blind tasting. All these surprises! Oh my goddess. How close is the wildfire?

Breathe Lena. Breathe.

"Wüter is refreshing. It's got minerals and tastes like real water. I drink it when Earth water is not available and during restrictions so I can take longer showers," I say practicing my line. My voice sounds surprisingly strong and doesn't waiver once.

The girl next to me, Sandy from Phoenix, smiles "That's what you're saying?"

"Yep," I gulp trying to act casual, "what's your line?"

"I play basketball for the Phoenix Wildcats. Smile. There is no Earth water left in Phoenix so I drink Wüter. It doesn't have hidden calories like sports drinks. Smile."

"Five minutes!" The director yells.

"You're not supposed to say smile," I tell Sandy from Phoenix. "You're just supposed to smile."

"Did I say smile?"

"Twice."

"Shoot."

Sandy gets quiet and closes her eyes. I do the same but not to practice my line.

"Denali!" I think.

"Hey, Lena! You okay?" he answers right away. I see a clear image of his concerned face, like he's been waiting.

"Where are you?"

"I'm in LA ... about to do the commercial. There's a wildfire headed our way and I still have to get my uncle and father in for recalibration. I don't know how much time I have. If I need you, are you around?"

"Absolutely! I was hoping to hear from you!"

"Thanks, I have no idea how this will go. I'm gonna try to do it alone but just like in case I need back up..."

"Hey! We're on the same team. I want to help. It's all about teamwork, okay?"

"One minute!" The director yells. "This is a live set! That

means there are no do overs. Speak slow and clear...if you make a mistake, repeat your line."

Set lights flood the stage. I blink. Am I going to lie to the world so my family can make more money?

"Three, two, one and action!"

"Welcome to a special edition of Channel Four News," Christine Torrino, the anchorwoman announces warmly with a perfect smile. "Tonight we're pleased to be the first to unveil a phenomenal scientific breakthrough that's going to chase away the water restriction blues. A wonderful new water substitute called Wüter hit the public stock market today. Interested investors should call within the hour to buy stock, it's going quickly and forecasted to be the biggest growing stock on the market in history. Yes, I said history."

"Wow, amazing Christine," says DeShawn Warner, the handsome anchorman next to her. He holds up a bottle of Wüter. "This stuff is absolutely amazing, have you tried it?"

For the next few minutes, I sweat out of every pore in my body watching actors, politicians, and news people gab about how great Wüter is, agonizing over whether I am going to recite my line or tell the truth. When Senator Paula Planco from New York speaks, I know I'm next.

The blood in my ears is pounding and although I try to listen to what the Senator is saying, all I hear is, "Wah wah wah...wah wah wah wah wah... Wüter wah thrilled ...wah wah wah New Yorkers never have to be thirsty again."

"Thank you, Senator," says DeShawn. "Now let's hear what our youngest panel member, Lena Linnigan from Wilmington, North Carolina has to say about Wüter. Lena's hometown Wilmington was just devastated by hurricane Ivanka, which not only caused extreme property damage, loss of homes and

flooding but oil and chemical spills so severe Wilmington

remains under level five water restrictions. Officials have no idea how long clean up will take."

"That is so sad, DeShawn," says anchorwoman Christine smiling. "Ms. Linnigan, tell us what you think of Wüter?"

The camera pans to me and I stare at myself staring at myself on screen. "I drink Wüter when Earth water is not avail- able," I say smiling. It has minerals and tastes like...(gulp) No. I hate Wüter! It tastes awful. *I want to drink real water, Christine not some substitute for the rest of my life.* You are right, this is sad! Sad and scary! Please!" I look straight into the camera and plead to the adults around the world, "Please, please clean up the water and stop using so much for things that aren't important so I...my generation and future generations can have a future to look forward to!"

"Ahh... are you sure that's how you feel?" Christine Torrino asks stunned, a perfect smile frozen on her face.

Sandy kicks me under the table.

"Whoop whoop whoop!" red lights flash and a loud whooping alarm sounds. "Whoop whoop whoop!"

A voice on the speaker booms, "Mandatory evacuation. Everyone must evacuate. The wildfire is one mile away. Winds are high and from the east, moving fast towards us. This is a mandatory evacuation. Everyone must evacuate immediately."

THIRTY-ONE

People scramble and stampede towards the door. I stand shakily and take off my microphone. Sandy and Senator Planco push past me knocking me to the floor. When I get up I see Uncle Leo and Dad screaming into their phones, shaking their heads pointing angry fingers at me.

"Everyone leave in a calm orderly fashion, the fire is one mile away, we have time to evacuate safely!" the director yells above the sudden din.

In the sea of fast moving bodies, I move towards my father and uncle.

"Dad!" I yell.

My angry father grabs my hand hard and pulls me in the opposite direction of the crowd.

Uncle Leo charges ahead of us like a mad bull, his face

imploding with rage. "My office!" he shouts. "We'll go out the side door."

"Follow your Uncle!" Dad pushes me behind Uncle Leo and we run to his plush office where he grabs his briefcase and holds his hand up to a safe.

"Start the car," he instructs my father. "I have a few words to say to your daughter while I empty the safe."

"Lena," my father says in a shaky voice, "You just cost us an enormous amount of money."

Uncle Leo tosses him the fob. My father opens the side door and steps out leaving me alone in the room with my uncle.

"Woop, woop, woop!" the fire alarm is getting louder and the building is beginning to feel hot. Out the window a curtain of thick, grey smoke darkens the sky.

"I'll just wait outside with Dad, okay?" I say sensing a greater danger than the fire brewing.

Uncle Leo keeps his back to me as he empties his safe, putting bags of silver and gold, and whatever else is in there into his briefcase.

"You little ingrate!" Uncle Leo suddenly growls turning around, eyes red and bulging. "You just cost me *billions of dollars*! Because of you, Wüter is going to die first day on the market! Do you know what that means for my reputation? For my business? I might have to sell Peekalo Island!"

Making the sound of a dying animal, my uncle grabs me by the shirt and throws me into the wall.

"Unnggh!" the air is knocked right out of me.

"Uncle Leo?" I cower, stunned. I've never seen a grown man so angry. Sinking to the ground, I gasp for breath and cover my head. "I just needed to ... tell the truth! Please...! I'm only fifteen!"

He pulls me up by the hair.

"Ahhhhh! Please don't hurt me, Uncle Leo! Daaaadddd!?" I scream as loud as I can.

The evacuation alarm is so loud it masks my scream.

"You're father is not going to help you. You ungrateful little shit. I could kill you." My uncle smashes my head against the wall again and my vision blurs. I taste blood and sink to the floor again. "Didn't anyone ever teach you? Never turn against family," he growls reaching for my neck this time.

I bite his hand as hard as I can. The taste of blood jolts me into action. I crawl quickly through his legs, grabbing the first thing I can that remotely resembles a weapon, a heavy glass paperweight on his desk. When he reaches for me again I hit him in the face with it as hard as I can.

The paperweight lands right on the bridge of his nose and I hear it crack. A stream of blood runs from his nose and drips off his chin onto the floor. He lunges for me again. I run around the desk straight for the door.

"Woop, woop, woop! Evacuate. Evacuate," the alarm blares in a robotic woman's voice.

My hand is on the doorknob. I am pulling it open as Uncle Leo catches my other arm. My fingers slip and he starts pulling me away. Like a lion, with my free hand I scratch at his eyes then jam my fingers right in the socket!

"Arghhrooo!!!!" he yells covering his eye with both hands.

I run out the door shaking, bloody, huffing and puffing. The fire is not a mile away anymore. It's here. Angry orange-red flames lick the sides of the building already digesting it. The cream colored siding fades to black as the sky blue awnings erupt in thick smoke snapping balls of fire and metal before melting into piles of ash on the asphalt.

Crackling, hissing heat pours off the burning building and the fire grows. My Uncle emerges from the building with his brief- case and broken, bloody nose.

"Denali!" I cry out my heart feeling as if it might burst.

In an instant Denali is beside me, the wind created by crack- ling flames blowing his silky black hair back, ash falling around him.

"Lena!?"

"But how did you do…" I start to ask, then seeing my Uncle moving towards us, "I need help!" I yell pointing at Uncle Leo. "Get my Uncle over here please! I'll get my Dad."

Crash! Bang. Bam. The largest awning on the building careens to the ground in a massive ball of flames and smoke.

"You mean the guy the burning awning just fell on?"

"Ohmygosh! Yes!"

"Dad, get out of the car!" I yell. "We need to help Uncle Leo!"

My father moves slowly, awkwardly not meeting my eyes or looking up, "All that money, gone," he mutters.

He gets out and stands limp by the car, like his soul has been sucked out of his body or something, while Denali and I pull my charred, bloody, passed out uncle from under the awning.

"Let's go now, Denali!" I grab my uncle and father's hands.

Denali and I lock eyes. I think with all my heart of Inner Earth. Of the circle we created and of the crystal cave entrance.

Now.

THIRTY-TWO

Flash, whir, and thick silence breaking through some gooey stuff and the four of us are in Inner Earth. My father and uncle fall in a heap to the shining grey floor, eyes rolling back into their heads. Two tall pale silvery blonde beings lift and whir them away on a hovering flat disc. I slump against Denali who supports me with a strong arm.

"Where are they taking my father and uncle?" I ask Arghata barely able to stand. "Can I see?"

"They will spend the next 24 hours quite comfortably in recalibration pods. It will feel like a nice refreshing, deep sleep, like a weekend at the spa."

"And when they wake up they'll be tuned to vibrate or uhhhm work with New Earth?"

"Precisely."

"Did they pass out because they're not Star Seeds so they can't travel in 5D?"

"Partially correct."

We walk down the grey slab hall a thousand or so feet to an elevator door, me leaning heavily on Denali. The door opens and we step in.

"Being a Star Seed just means you were born with a particular mission to fulfill, a particular task to complete. There are many Star Seeds on Earth today. The exact number in the high hundred thousands I would guess. Less than 1% of these Star Seeds are traveling bridge communicators, however. Which is a rare, high calling indeed. It means you vibrate at the highest frequency available for a soul in a human body. You can thank your maternal ancestors for that."

I think we go down two levels while Arghata is speaking but I can't be sure. I am so tired and woozy. The door opens and we step out. This level is much different. Everything, I mean everything here is white.

"Welcome to the 5D heart chakra level where all recalibration takes place. There are 444 pods here and they are all in use. It is a very busy time. Your father and uncle are in pods 111 and 112. They just opened today. Couldn't have been better timing."

My mouth falls open and my eyes widen. The three of us step into the white. I can't see anything.

"Your eyes will adjust."

As we walk, clear magenta outlines of numbered oval pods begin taking shape to my right and left. The light turns from a blinding white to a softer golden white. I am vaguely aware of a high frequency sound.

"Here are your father and uncle. Safe and sound in their pods."

I blink. Dad and Uncle Leo are in there already?

Stepping away from the stable, supportive, warm frame of Denali, I lean into pod number 111. It is cool with a thin layer

of ice on top. There is a small window where I vaguely make out my fathers sleeping face. On the side, an electro meter of some sort reads 1% complete. I lean into 112 and I see the top of Uncle Leo's bald head. His face is turned away from me. He is at .05%.

"But how did they get in there so fast?" I ask astonished.

"You do not need to know the details of everything dear. You yourself have been here longer than you realize."

A surge of immense satisfaction washes over me seeing my father and uncle resting peacefully in recalibration pods and then... I see a glimpse of the future. A vision. The sign on Dad's office which currently says, "Linnigan and Mackey: We Fight for Big Business" now says "Linnigan and Mackey: We Fight for Earth."

"Did you have a vision my dear?"

"Ya, a good one... I... I saw the sign on my father's office change from, we fight for big business to we fight for Earth." I turn to Arghata stunned.

"You seem excited about that."

"Oh, I am. Thanks for putting them next to each other. Will they remember any of this?"

"They will remember only deep sleep."

Three tall pale blondes in white and silver clothing float past us to pod number 118. A young looking fish creature flaps along behind them, checking each monitor methodically, adjusting numbers as needed.

I slump into Denali again, officially exhausted. He puts a

protective arm around me. "You need rest."

"Yes, rest and regain strength," says Arghata. "It will not be long until your next mission..."

AFTERWORD

Thank you for reading *Star Seed Nation*. I love hearing from readers. Sharon@Sharveda.com

Made in the USA
Coppell, TX
06 October 2020

39395099R00157